MURDER TAKES THE BATHS

by

LEE PRIESTLEY

Thermal Springs, where the old and crippled came for the curative baths, was hardly an exciting place. But since Ellen Knowles felt dragged out and had aching joints after a year attempting to teach the niceties of English literature to sixteen-year-olds, the quiet spa town seemed a wise if hardly a thrilling choice of a vacation site.

The baths proved as invigorating as the attentions of lanky Tom Ranger, a visiting Texan, proved pleasing and palatable. In fact, Ellen would gladly have let things stand there.

Instead, an old lady was drowned in the baths, and Ellen was suddenly a link in a murder chain—hardly a remedy for relaxing tension. Since Tom was by profession a homicide expert, he tried to help out, but even his skill could not keep the curious and too-knowing Ellen from putting her neck in constant danger.

An unusual setting provides the background for a highly suspenseful and readable mystery.

MURDER TAKES THE BATHS

Murder Takes the Baths

by
LEE PRIESTLEY

WILDSIDE PRESS

www.wildsidepress.com

MURDER TAKES THE BATHS

CHAPTER I

"The Gobi Desert couldn't be hotter," Ellen Knowles muttered grimly, lifting a hand to steady the wet towel wrapped around her head.

A wave of fiery water crested at her movement and she looked incredulously at the thermometer hovering near one hundred degrees; the water felt twice that hot. She couldn't sit still and parboil, but her slightest squirm lapped the mineral bath over skin that shrank from the contact. Then the shrinking launched more ripples and the ripples outraged more areas of epidermis. So the bath progressed in a vicious circle of flinching and scalding.

Ellen cursed the twinging shoulder that had led her to undertake the series of baths. The remedy was certainly far worse than the disease. Shutting her teeth, she shifted gingerly from one hip to the other. The effort brought tears to her eyes. The water was pure liquid fire. She bit back a yell as the red hot waves lapped on her shoulders. Her head ached from the steamy heat, and the soft, intermittent rasping from the next cubicle was as irritating as a fingernail drawn over sandpaper.

"And I'm paying good money to be tortured like this!" she groaned aloud.

"Yes, miss, I know you are," a rich, throaty voice agreed. "But you're goin' to feel lots better when we get through with you."

The figure in the doorway would have made Ellen start if she hadn't remembered in time the results of sudden movement in the steaming water. The Negro woman might have stepped down from the frieze of an Egyptian temple to bring a libation of ice water in a paper cup. She was wrapped in a tan cotton shift held in place by a fold and a twist that reached over one shoulder to leave both arms bare, and ended high up on the middle-aged, spindly legs. Her feet were thrust half in, half out of tattered paper slippers.

When the cup was emptied, the Egyptian held up a large sheet and waited patiently. Ellen looked at the time indicator.

"The doctor told me to stay in fifteen minutes," she said reluctantly. "That thing shows just ten minutes past."

"Yassum, you're supposed to stay the full time, but I let my ladies out early the first day till they get hardened to it more." The attendant sniffed scornfully. "What do those doctors know about how hot this water gets? They don't take these baths." She deftly wrapped the sheet about Ellen's steaming body, then directed, "Just step out, miss, and lie down on that last cot there at the end of the room."

Ellen had been directed by the desk clerk to the cubicle where she had left her clothes and then had been ushered into Number Fourteen. She had no more than a glance into the room that opened from the bath hall. Now she walked down a strip of wet rubber matting into an assemblage of steaming ghosts. They trailed clutched sheets as she did and were harried along by more Egyptians who bedded them down on rattan couches.

Ellen's couch was one of a long row occupied by women of all ages and sizes. On one side her neighbor was a tiny, wizened old woman with a face like a brown nut; beyond her little figure loomed a woman of mountainous obesity. On the last couch lay a young woman whose towel-wrapped profile was madonna-like. On the other side, the woman ranged from middle to old age as nearly as she could judge from the visible crow's-feet and double chins. They lay quietly and without much talk, wiping their faces constantly with the cold towel ends. Ellen, too, lay still and steamed, grateful for the cracked ice.

The drowsy silence was broken by a small colored woman emerging from a cubicle at the end of the row of couches with the suddenness of an apparition. She chanted in a loud voice, "Twenty-nine for Bella, twenty-nine for Bella."

No one moved or seemed to pay any attention. The woman repeated, "Twenty-nine for Bella, twenty-nine for Bella." Then she added patiently, "Well, one of you ladies is twenty-nine for Bella!" Her eyes fixed on Ellen. "What did your card say, miss?"

Ellen felt completely stupid as she realized that the card she had been given at the desk had indeed "said" twenty-nine for Bella. She sat up on her couch, making a belated snatch at her sheet disappearing over the edge to the floor. The woman beckoned with impatience and returned to her box. Ellen walked past the reclining row to its doorway.

The box proved to be the massage room. "Lie down, miss," Bella directed briskly, indicating a short rubber-covered shelf that nearly filled the tiny room. "On your back, please."

The protecting sheet was snatched away then, but Bella dropped a towel as a sop to modesty. She reached for a bottle on a shelf and filled her hands with a liquid smelling loudly of wintergreen, camphor, and alcohol. She began to thump and rub and slap Ellen vigorously. The thumps and spats stopped just short of hurting and soon the parboiled skin began to glow. Ellen was told to turn over on her stomach and the thumping went on with even more vigor, since on that side of a lady nature has provided a section perfect for swatting.

Winding up with a crescendo that involved thuds, slaps, the travelling up and down her back of the edges of Bella's hands and a final clap at the back of her neck, Ellen was pronounced finished. She sat up obediently, clutching automatically at the retreating towel. Bella held her sheet for her as she climbed off the shelf.

As she walked back along the rubber matting past the waiting women, Ellen felt like a handful of over-cooked spaghetti. She wondered how she would ever endure twenty more ordeals like this first one. Reach-

ing the cell where she had left her clothes, she dropped
the sheet and collapsed weakly on the corner seat.
She groaned when she remembered that she had
agreed to everything that young Doctor Doulton had
proposed for the relief of the rheumatic shoulder.
The schedule of examinations and tests and treatments
stretched out endlessly in her mind's eye.

What was she doing here anyway? she asked herself
tartly. Anybody would feel dragged out and achey
at the end of a year of attempting to teach literature
to hundreds of sixteen-year-olds whose interests, she
knew, and whose abilities, she feared, did not rise
above Dick Tracy. Why hadn't she left well enough
alone? Her shoulder would probably have felt normal
again of its own accord without the elaborate routine
to which she was now committed.

Or, if she must take baths, why hadn't she picked
out a more interesting place in which to take them?
Her first glimpses of Thermal Springs had not been
promising. A coffee-colored station with an Oriental
twist to the roof, a large sign no doubt of Chamber of
Commerce inspiration identifying the stop as "Thermal Springs, Where America Bathes for Radiant
Health!" and taxi drivers competing for her luggage.

"Which hotel, miss?" the winner had asked.

Ellen hadn't known, so they had taken a look at
what was offered. Every other house along the tree-
lined streets had a Board and Room sign with a wheel
chair ramp conveniently placed beside the front steps.
As they drove, the taxi driver recommended the
Thermal, and she had approached it to the accom-

paniment of his chatter about the number of rooms in its five stories, its modernity and the superiority of its bathhouse.

Having a feminine desire to shop around, Ellen had asked to see the other hotel, despite the driver's assurance that it couldn't compare with the splendors he had just described. "Why, it ain't even got a cocktail lounge, miss, if you can believe it," he said, and was amazed that that lack didn't seem to impress his passenger unduly.

"There's the Eureka," he had said disdainfully at the end of the next block.

The Eureka did look antique, but Ellen had liked the look. Set back in a green rim, its white pillars ran up to a second story balcony on either side and provided a shady veranda well populated with rocking chairs.

"There are probably cockroaches in the bathrooms," she told the driver, "but I'm not really modern either."

"It's kinda famous for its food," the man conceded, knowing that his chance for his dollar from the Thermal was gone anyway. "That'll be sixty-five cents."

Her room was bright with chintz and the bed was good. The bath shone with new tile, but there the modernization ended. The furniture was appallingly heavy walnut and there was that faint mousy odor that all old houses acquire and which the lovers of the antique sniff with pleasure rather than censure. A stiff bouquet of zinnias stood in the exact center of a marble-topped table standing in turn in the exact center of the room. Ellen felt completely at home.

Later, as she put on her hat to start her shoulder on its tour of the clinic, she had looked at her reflection in the wavy old mirror and wondered what made the taxi driver think a cocktail lounge was essential to anyone who looked as schoolteacherish as she did. The glass showed her dark hair pulled back into an uninspired bun, brown eyes under arching brows that she considered her only beauty, a generous mouth apt to be held primly above a determined chin. (You have to be determined to have any discipline in high school if you are only five feet one.) Practical navy sheer suit, panama hat about as dashing as a peach basket, arch preserver shoes. She bent closer to powder her nose and ceased to look critically at herself. It was the same Ellen she was used to seeing. The taxi driver should learn to size people up better.

The desk clerk had told her there was a clinic next door or another down the street near the Thermal Hotel. He could recommend either one, he assured her. Ellen didn't expect to hear anything new or alarming, for her own doctor had examined her thoroughly. It seemed highly unlikely that either clinic would fail to prescribe the baths for which the town was famous. So, she had concluded, why walk in the heat any farther than next door?

Heat from the pavements was scorching waves that visibly beat against her face. She had ducked into the dim corridor and inspected the directory beside the elevator. From the doctors she had chosen "Doctor Paul Lysander Doulton, Jr.," because the name went trippingly on the tongue, and considered that as good a way as any to choose.

The doctor's waiting room was filled, but the alert receptionist catalogued Ellen and found her a chair before she could make up her mind not to wait. She had liked Doctor Doulton's taste in decoration; it was pleasant to find a waiting room in Early American rather than Late Grand Rapids or Transition Chromium Pipe. Some of the pieces were old and all the reproductions were good. Ellen definitely coveted the arrow back chair on which she sat and a hobnail celery vase on a hanging shelf. So she had waited.

Still farther impressed by the blond good looks of the young doctor, she had found him serious and sympathetic about the shoulder. Soon she had a card with a bewilderingly complete list of appointments with specialists and dentists and X-ray technicians. And, of course, a card for twenty-one of the baths that were practically guaranteed. She remembered that she had felt reassured and certain that the twinges were doomed.

All of that, Ellen thought gloomily as she reached for a stocking, had been before she had taken the first bath. So here she was, sitting on a shelf, as bare as the day she was born, with twenty more sessions of being boiled to a rag and pounded to a pulp looming ahead. She languidly finished dressing and made a few ineffectual pokes at her thoroughly cowed hair. Leaving a tip at the desk for Bella, the rubber, she emerged into the hot white sunshine at the bath house door. Across the street a soda fountain invited the newly bathed,

and Ellen decided that part of her limpness was probably an empty stomach. A soda would fortify her until
she could try the food for which the Eureka was
famous.

Opening the screen into the antiseptic dimness of
the drug store, she caromed from an emerging cus-
tomer and brushed a bundle to the floor. "I'm sorry,"
Ellen said, stooping to pick up the parcel which had
clanged on the tile floor at her feet. "I didn't see you
at all. In fact, I can't see a thing yet; it's that awful
glare."

Her eyes beginning to adjust to the dimness, she
held out the package, knobby and stuck together with
a gummed tape bearing some merchant's advertising.
"I hope it hasn't been damaged and if—"

Her voluble apology was interrupted by a hand
reaching out to snatch at the package. Ellen's focusing
eyes saw only a blue linen back walking rapidly away.

She felt a little dashed at the silent reception of all
her words. Surely the woman could have said, "It's
quite all right," without using up all her conversation
for the day. At a damp, marble-topped table, Ellen,
spooned a chocolate sundae and realized crossly that
the bath had made her feel very well indeed.

CHAPTER II

Ellen couldn't believe her eyes when she looked at her watch. It had been barely three o'clock when she had undressed for the third time that day and decided to take a short nap. Now the timepiece insisted that it was eight o'clock. The relaxing bath had been responsible for that deep five hour sleep.

Looking at the dark silk suit, she decided she was tired of pushing herself in and out of it. She chose a light thin print from the short sensible row in her closet and re-read the hotel's rules as she buttoned and zipped. The fact that the dining room positively closed at seven-thirty made her even hungrier.

She was dismayed when the elevator projected her into a lobby reception complete with dressed up women and a punch bowl on a flower-decorated table. Her second glance as she hurriedly turned toward the street door was intercepted by a busy little woman who trotted toward her with outstretched hands and a firmly friendly smile. "What in this world—?" Ellen asked herself.

"You're a new guest, aren't you, dear?" the glossy little woman pounced. Upon Ellen's murmur of agreement, she was turned about, her arm cozily linked in the other's. "I'm so glad I saw you in time! It's such an opportunity to meet all these nice people and feel right at home from the start. We are just like a big family here, and we want you to have the best vacation with us! I want you to know dear Mrs. Horton; and Miss Dixon and—oh, how are you, Mrs. Bryce? I hadn't seen you today. You mustn't neglect me! Now what did you say your name is, dear?"

Ellen identified herself and was propelled around the lobby. She got a confused impression of middle-aged female faces swimming in a sea of commercial heartiness. Occasionally a face would vary the pattern by belonging to a pair of trousers instead of a suitable summer print. These exceptions received extra and coy attentions from the chattering hostess.

Even large families come to an end, so Ellen was at last permitted to sit on the edge of a chair too deep for her and make polite conversation. She might have escaped then, for her perch was near the hall door, had she not hungrily accepted the plate and punch cup. The small, dapper man who handed it to her then sat down chummily on a footstool in front of her.

"Sweets to the sweet," he beamed with an air of great originality and, taking off his rimless glasses, he polished them vigorously. "When Dora captured you there at the elevators I knew you'd be just my type. How long do you plan to stay in Thermal Springs? Years, I hope."

Ellen blinked. "I bet you say that to all the girls,"

she countered feebly.

A hoarse chuckle from the other side startled her. The tall woman in a nurse's uniform who sat there regarded Ellen's middle-aged wolf with malice in her sharp eyes. "He certainly does," she said in a husky voice. "That's been his opening gambit for the last ten years, and I, for one, am heartily sick of hearing it! Can't you give that old chestnut a rest, Hamp?"

"Oh, come now, Miss Liz, you're too hard on me," the man protested. "You always refuse my attentions, but you don't want me to hover around the new blossoms."

The sharp eyes regarded him again from an angle as the woman's gray, elaborately curled head tipped to one side. "That's it!" she said with huge satisfaction. "That's what you've always reminded me of—a bee buzzing around."

The woman's hands that had been twining and twisting in her lap began to describe airy circles. Ellen, feeling that her mouth had dropped open, shut it firmly as her fascinated eyes followed the fingers now circling in wider and wider arcs around the woman's head.

"Now, Miss Liz," the man said soothingly, but somewhat shaken in his jaunty manner, "that's hardly a flattering comparison."

"Didn't intend it to be," the woman said ferociously. "I hate bees!" Pulling herself to her feet, she stood looking down at Ellen, then stabbed at her with a long finger. "Stay away from bees! Nasty self-centered creatures. Besides, they sting."

She stalked off across the lobby to stand punching

the elevator button. Bewildered, Ellen looked around her. Apparently no one had paid any attention to the scene. She clutched at the arms of the enfolding chair, determined to leave while her sanity lasted. A plump white hand descended on her fingers and patted maternally.

"Dear Miss Knowles, please, *please* don't be disturbed." It was the consciously sweet voice of the hostess. "Although I'm sure it's best that you know about our skeleton in the closet at once. Don't you think so, Hampton? But really I don't know what possessed me to call dear Miss Liz such a dreadful thing! She's certainly no skeleton and we couldn't keep her in a closet if we tried; she just goes wherever and whenever she pleases. She was the head nurse in the Clinic here for many years, Miss Knowles, and now that she is—" the voice paused delicately to choose a phrase—"somewhat clouded in intellect, dear Doctor Doulton won't hear of having her confined. Of course the poor dear's perfectly harmless," the hostess reassured Ellen. "Just a bit odd at times. And she has no relatives and no other home—"

"She called me a bee, Dora," Hampton said in an aggrieved voice. "She said I buzzed!"

Ellen resisted an impulse to laugh in his hurt face. He did look like a bee. There was that deadly serious aspect of industry on his round countenance. Woolly eyebrows over protuberant, multiple eyes, the faintly distracted air of the worker in enforced idleness. His well brushed, crinkly black hair completed the illusion.

"Of course you don't buzz," Dora Martingale told

him soothingly. "But you mustn't pay any attention to the poor old thing. She doesn't know what she says half the time and the other half she doesn't mean it." She turned her facile smile on Ellen again. "I hope you won't let this upset you, dear. Poor Hampton! Miss Liz gets quite sharp with him, and I'm sure no one can understand it. That's not the way we all feel!" Her smile was as inviting as an open syrup jug, and the man basked in its sweetness. "Come help me a minute, Hampton?"

Well! Ellen said mentally. As she sat back in the chair again she noticed the plate with canapé and cake and punch cup that she still held. As she feared, it proved to be an anemic anchovy and a chocolate cake looking and tasting like a plug of Old Granger.

No one seemed interested in her for the moment. On one side the empty chair protected her, on the other two women were comparing notes about the wrong ways their daughters-in-law were raising their grandchildren. Ellen slipped away to find that nearly an hour had been consumed in the family party and that the cafés on the hotel street had closed unanimously. She walked down the street past the Thermal and its bath house, but the town did not keep late hours. Even the drugstores had locked up their sandwiches and sodas. The only prospect was the popcorn stand in the movie lobby.

Ellen enjoyed her food, and the thought of an early breakfast did nothing to assuage the pangs of hunger. Glumly turning toward the popcorn, she reflected that the first day of this vacation, if you could

call it such, had been disappointing. Then next door
to the movie, half hidden by its glaring lights, she saw
that she was passing Harry's Hamburger Hut, empty
of customers, but still open. She opened the door and
walked in hurriedly before it too retired for the
night. After all, she thought, one could always take a
little bicarb.

In her haste she trod upon a furry huddle that
shrieked in outrage and held up a damaged paw
piteously. A very pretty girl popped up from a stool
around a corner of the counter to croon to the spaniel;
a redheaded waiter appeared from nowhere; a cook
with a spatula in his hand leaned out of his cubbyhole
kitchen to ask indignantly why she couldn't look
where she was going. Ellen sat down firmly on the
nearest stool and stilled the uproar by apologizing in
turn to the dog, the girl, the waiter and the cook.
Then she ordered their biggest Pore Boy sandwich.

It proved to be twelve inches of food. A long roll,
split and fortified with mustard, held a slab of bar-
becued beef, sliced onions, lettuce and tomato, and a
villainous-looking sauce. She went to work hungrily
while she got acquainted with the four. Pete, the
counter boy, went to High where he played football.
The cook had once worked in Ellen's home town.
The pretty girl and the spaniel were Susan and Brown
Sugar, librarians. Ellen even knew Susan's guilty secret. She had been propped on an elbow behind the
coffee urn engrossed in a hamburger with onions and
"The Stony-faced Corpse."

Ellen laughed and admitted to a liking for the lesser

forms of literature. Susan companionably moved herself, the book and the remaining half-moon of hamburger to a front stool, while Brown Sugar, the spaniel, graciously accepted bites of the Pore Boy, raking delicately with a fringed forepaw when the intervals seemed too long. Looking from Sugar to her mistress, Ellen saw with a glint of amusement that girl and dog resembled each other.

Susan caught the glance and smiled. "I think we look alike, too," she said. "Only Sugar's far more beautiful and her pedigree's more impressive." The girl shook curling red brown hair from eyes that were big, deep brown and expressive. Where Sugar's eyes were mournful, Susan's eyes were merry. "I'm thinking of teaching her to read and then no one will be able to tell us apart. Only what happens to me shouldn't happen to a dog," she added gloomily.

Ellen was interested. "Why shouldn't it?"

"Look at me," Susan commanded bitterly. "Absolutely nothing's happened to me in my whole life! Years and years I've been the only inhabitant under the age of sixty. All the boys grow up and go away. All the girls—except me—grow up to be secretaries or bubble dancers, or anyhow get married. Susan keeps right on being a good girl and staying with Grandmother. She's a darling, but I ask you. Nothing ever happens. When my grandchildren—if I ever have any—ask me, 'Tell us about the exciting days when you were young, Grandma,' I'll have to say, 'Grandma recommended hot love stories to housewives, darlings, and got this stiff arm from stamping due dates!' "

Ellen laughed. "Probably a very useful work, keeping up the housewives' spirits."

"But what it did to mine. I don't think I could have stood it much longer if he—" She bent to give Sugar a bite of onion from her plate. The little dog sniffed it and looked at her mistress reproachfully.

Ellen poked at the remains in her own plate. When Susan did not continue, she said, "I'm not sure I like it here myself. I don't know why, but I've felt apprehensive ever since I arrived. It's just what I expected: the usual peaceful small town where everything revolves around the hotels and bath houses and where everyone is preoccupied with his health. Nevertheless, I feel as fey as my Scotch grandmother. I believe if it wasn't for that same ancestress I'd leave tomorrow."

Susan's eyebrows wondered about the connection between going home and a Scotch ancestress.

"I've paid my hotel and bath house bill in advance," Ellen said dryly.

"Thermal Springs is really funny," Susan said. "You know, not funny ha! ha! but funny peculiar." Forsaking her serious mood, she leveled a forefinger menacingly at Ellen. "Believe me, Madam, you have entered a crazy, twenty-one-day microcosm!"

The dire effect of the warning was somewhat spoiled by Sugar sitting up to whiff at the pointing forefinger. Ellen laughed. "I think I'll chance it."

"There's no telling what will happen," Susan predicted darkly.

With a crash that stopped the beating of Ellen's

heart a heavy missile smashed through the front window of Harry's Hamburger Hut and swept Susan from her stool. She lay where she had fallen while the little dog whined and licked her face and a last piece of glass tinkled to the floor.

CHAPTER III

The occupants of Harry's Hamburger Hut were turned to stone. Pete clutched the cup he was drying while the freckles came out on his white face like stars at dusk; the cook leaned on the pie case with his mouth open; Ellen sat with a bite of sandwich caught in her throat by a gasp of astonishment.

The front door flew open and bounced against the wall. A tall young man thrust the hair out of his eyes and demanded, "Anybody get hurt? What the devil's going on anyway?" Then he saw Susan on the floor.

The Hamburger Hut came to life again. Pete vaulted the counter, dropping towel and cup; the cook swore volubly; and Ellen remembered from a First Aid course that you never gave a stimulant to an unconscious person. But efficiency had arrived with the ruffled young man. While he deftly examined the small cut oozing red on Susan's forehead, he sent Pete for a basin and cold water, directed the cook to phone for the night policeman and told Ellen to get that dog out of the way. Following his orders, she felt surprise at the experienced way the young man lifted Susan's eyelids and gently ran his hands over her head.

Then he lifted the girl to a semi-sitting position against his knees and looked up. "She's all right," he said. "Probably have a headache, and I sent for the basin in case— Hey, Pete! Hustle up!"

Susan had opened her eyes and looked mistily about her. Then she turned an alarming green and, coordinating with Pete's return over the counter with the basin, was violently sick. When the paroxysm was over she said weakly, "How awful of me! What am I doing on the floor, Sandy?"

Then Ellen recognized Sandy as the dignified young doctor of her clinic experience. Sandy from the Lysander, of course. That accounted for the way he had handled things.

"Someone heaved a brick through the window and caught you quite a clip," he was explaining to Susan, indignation visible on his face and audible in his voice. "When I came around the corner across the street, I saw someone flattened beside the window, looking in. Seemed queer, so I stopped under the shadow of an awning to see what was up. The guy bent over, snatched up a brick from that construction next door, threw it and ran. I went right after him, but I didn't have a prayer. Time I got to the end of the alley, he'd had time to hide forty places. So I came back to see if anybody'd got hit."

Susan moved against his knee. "Golly, I didn't know anybody felt like hitting me with a brick." She looked up into the doctor's face, and Ellen observed that she did something demure with her eyelashes. "I don't believe anyone knows me well enough to want to murder me. Maybe they planned to bump me, not to bump me off." She explored the rising goose egg with cautious fingers. "Don't you think we've sat on the floor long enough, Sandy?"

As the young doctor bent to lift Susan to her feet he agreed to Harry's proposal of coffee on the house. When it came, Ellen recalled herself to him and told him of Susan's prophetic warning.

Sandy laughed grimly. "She's mighty right. This is a screwy place. It didn't seem queer to me when I was growing up, but since I've been back— I don't know whether it's the town or me. I don't think I'd stay if Dad wasn't killing himself running the place practically single-handed. Why, the crazy feud between Dad and that bird Fowler is enough to unsettle the reason! I swear, Susan, I thought they'd come to blows at the Chamber of Commerce dinner last night."

"Doctor Fowler, of the Thermal Hotel and Bath House," Susan cleared up the reference. "And determined to have all the patients by fair means or Fowler."

"Now I know you ought to get that bump to bed," Sandy told her, laughing. "But that guy makes me mad enough to spit between my teeth. Fowler exchanges the merest chit-chat with the condescension of a king addressing his kennel keeper, and if we try to talk shop with him he implies we're so old-fashioned and obsolete that we practice bleeding."

Nobody said anything, and Harry leaned out to refill their cups. Then he rested on the pie case, plying a toothpick and asking around it, "Doc Fowler ain't really hurt your Dad, has he, Sandy?"

Sandy nodded. "Some, Harry. It's not as if our patients here were permanent people. Folks come and go, and there's no time to correct first impressions. Fowler's done quite a job of making us look like a lot of fuddy-duddy old horse doctors."

"You seem a little young for a fuddy-duddy," Susan murmured.

Sandy stirred his coffee thoughtfully. "Of course there's never a thing you can put your finger on. He's too smart for that."

"He's too smart, period," Susan told Ellen. "You know a manner composed of the very best butter? It ought to put anyone on their guard with the man at once."

"It doesn't, though," Sandy said wearily. "He certainly appeals to the girls at least. That personal magnetism—ha!—and those shiny tile and chromium baths are making it very tough on the old Eureka."

"The Eureka has atmosphere," Susan said loyally.

"And mice, too," Sandy added.

"It's really a pretty good old dump, Doc," Harry argued. "And the food's better'n anything for miles. My cousin Ernie that's head cook gets offers from all over."

" Is that a fact?" Sandy asked. "By George, we'll raise his wages a little for sticking with the ship."

"Come on, Miss Ellen. Let's go home," Susan said, "before Sandy starts weeping into that cup of cold coffee."

"Who's weeping into what cup?" Sandy glared at

her. "Harry asked me and I told him."

"Everything will work out, Doc." Harry's tone was soothing. "You and your Dad are great guys and everybody in town knows it."

"But that's just what I've been telling you, Harry. It doesn't make any difference what everybody in town knows. The bulk of any health resort doctor's practice comes from out of town." He smoothed his hair and apparently his temper at the same time. "Come on, gals. Let's get going."

After they had talked with the night policeman, who clucked like a disapproving hen over the brick heaving, the three walked slowly toward the hotel and Susan's grandmother's house. The schoolteacher's eyes in the back of her head that Ellen had developed by years of practice bothered her. She had a persistent feeling that there was someone behind them.

With amusement she told herself that they were being "shadowed" as she watched their elongated silhouettes advance ahead of them. Then she turned her attention to what Sandy and Susan were saying.

"So many of the patients are bad-tempered and crotchety," Sandy remarked. "In spite of myself I resent them, even when I know that a saint couldn't endure their pain and keep sweet. Which reminds me," he said to Susan, "the Chathams started through the Clinic again today."

"I know," Susan said. "Grandmother asked them to supper last night. They got in yesterday. I was just thinking that they are a perfect example of what I was telling Miss Ellen back at the Hut. They've been com-

ing here every summer for years. There's old Miss
Sara—Sandy, she's getting awfully old. Is she going to
take the baths again?—and Mr. Charles, only he's accidental, not arthritic. And Miss Isobel, poor darling,
and Denise who just comes along for the ride.

"And just to prove everybody knows everything,"
Susan giggled, "the switchboard girl told the bath
house clerk, and one of the rubbers heard her and told
Grandmother's cook, that the lobby sitters thought
Denise and Sandy made the best-looking couple, and
they wouldn't be a bit surprised!"

Sandy muttered about gossiping old hens.

"Of course it's nobody's business if you take Denise
out," Susan agreed. "They only notice it. The reason
I mentioned it was to show Miss Ellen how everybody
knows everything."

The lobby held only four persons sitting by a window instead of the big family of an hour before. One
of them was the indefatigable hostess, who nimbly got
back on the job as they entered.

"What a quick worker you are, Miss Knowles!" she
chattered, with an arch look for Sandy. "You leave
here a perfect stranger and come back escorted by our
handsomest young man. Do come meet two more of
our guests. They really are family! We are so glad to
welcome them back, for we just wouldn't know what
to do without them!"

"No doubt go into the red at the Clinic," said the
man toward whom Ellen was being steered.

"Why, Mr. Charles, how can you think us so mer-
cenary? Miss Knowles, Mr. Charles Chatham and

Denise. And you've met Hampton, you remember?"

Ellen would have found the Chathams interesting even if she hadn't heard about them. Pain and temper showed in the lines of the man's face and intelligence looked from his sharp violet eyes. His head, with a dramatic shock of silver hair springing from a high forehead, would have graced a Roman coin. He acknowledged the introduction in a sonorous voice, but he did not rise nor seem to see the hand Ellen had extended.

As Ellen turned to speak to Denise, a careful glance showed her the man's hands twisted and misshapen under the robe that covered his knees and concealed the lower part of the wheel chair in which he sat. She felt a pang of pity for him, chained like an eagle to a rock.

But delectable was the word for Denise. Tall, golden, violet-eyed, she was the most dazzling thing Ellen had ever seen. To say that she was beautiful was rank understatement. The dark slacks that she wore revealed a body as lovely as her face. As she stood beside her uncle the contrast between her young grace and his twisted, racked frame was painful. Her polite words of greeting over, she turned to Susan and Sandy.

Sandy explained the white plaster on Susan's forehead amid excited twittering from Miss Martingale, the hostess, and Hampton Potts.

"But Susan, darling! you might have been killed!" Miss Martingale shuddered dramatically. "I told Hampton just yesterday—you remember I did, don't

you, Hampton?—that everything was just going from
bad to worse. And now this terrible attack!"

"Really, Miss Dora, I'm not hurt," Susan said, "and
it wasn't an attack, I'm sure. I don't think the brick
could have been meant for me."

"You can't believe anyone would dislike you
enough to smack you down, Sue? Well, I doubt it
myself, you're so sweet." Denise smiled a little twist-
edly. "I'll bet there are plenty people would love to
bop me a good one!"

"Don't brag, Denise," her uncle said dryly. "But
Susan does seem an odd target for anything except
Cupid's arrows perhaps."

"If it was Cupid, he's changed his armament." Sandy
smiled at the little librarian. Ellen had thought Susan
a very pretty girl, but beside the stunning Denise, she
looked almost plain. Was there a touch of winter in
the smile curving Denise's red mouth and in the glance
she gave Susan?

"Come on, darling; let's get you home. I'll go along,
for Sandy has to come back anyway, and you look so
pale and washed out he may need me to tuck you in."
Denise put an arm around Susan and, Ellen noticed,
maneuvered her away from Sandy.

As she watched them go out while she waited for
the elevator, Ellen thought Denise extinguished Susan's appealing prettiness as a neon sign overpowers a
candle.

CHAPTER IV

Eight-thirty next morning found Ellen eating her way through the breakfast menu with enthusiasm. As she watched butter melting in a golden pool on a mound of grits, she told herself that a woman of her age looked better with well padded bones. Then she protested the habitual thought—at her age. How old was thirty-four? Hardly senility. Perhaps her grandmother admonishing the lonely child Ellen "to be a big girl" had made her age conscious. There had been nothing very young about the bookish Ellen growing up in a world of her grandmother's contemporaries, or about the present Ellen, head of an English department and being groomed for dean of girls at her mid-western school. The years ahead followed regimented ruts, and her lips curled with distaste. Then she shook her head, dismissing her uncomfortable thoughts. What was the matter with her?

The dining room was nearly empty; apparently few of the guests felt hearty enough for an early breakfast. She smiled vaguely at a face or two that looked familiar, probably from the mass introduction of the night before. Then she decided against more hot biscuits with fig preserves, not because she couldn't have eaten them, but because the colored waiters had been eyeing her plate with astonishment for some time. She pushed back her chair.

The lobby was deserted except for a maid who languidly pushed a mop around the feet of a tall man folded into a chair reading the *El Paso Times*. As she waited for the elevator, Ellen wondered how the reader of the *Times* could walk in the high-heeled, sharp-toed cowboy boots he was wearing. The footgear were works of art in stitched and intricately tooled leather, but they didn't look comfortable.

When the elevator doors slid open they discharged Doctor Sandy and another white-coated physician enough like him to make Ellen sure of his identity before she heard his name. The senior Doctor Doulton had given Sandy his dancing grey eyes, and their rumpled blond heads were the same, the older man's dusted with gray.

At Sandy's introduction, Doctor Doulton said mildly, "I must say you don't look like the kind of person who would get involved in a riot at a hamburger stand."

Ellen protested, "Not a riot, Doctor. Just a—" She searched for a word.

"Just a Pore Boy with mustard and mayhem?"

Ellen laughed and asked Sandy how Susan was. He reported that she would spend the morning at home with a pretty severe headache, but was otherwise all right. "She looked as pitiful as a battered baby with that sticking plaster on her forehead," he added. "The chief of police was patting her hand and promising war at the very least when I saw her."

Ellen noticed that the reader of the *El Paso Times* had dropped his paper to listen, unabashed, to their conversation. As her severe glance caught his, he extracted his length from the chair and approached them, his hand outstretched to the older doctor.

"Howdy, Doc," he said, grinning. "I can't stand it any longer. What in time are you three talking about?"

"How are you, Tom?" The doctor shook hands with a chuckle. "I might have known you'd scent violence." Turning to Ellen, he said, "Miss Knowles, this is Tom Ranger. He claims he works for the city of Dallas, head man for homicide, but you can see he's just a frustrated cowhand." The doctor stared down pointedly at the enormous, hand-made boots.

Ellen's hand was engulfed and heartily shaken. "Good mornin', Miss Knowles. I am kinda curious about the fight last night," the man said earnestly, "but I really wanted a chance to meet you. I watched you in the dining room a while ago and made up my mind."

"But why, for gracious sake?" Ellen was puzzled, her eyes searching his tanned, angular face.

"I tell you, I get so sick of watching these ladies pick and putter at their meals! When I saw you eating breakfast, I told myself, there's a woman with enough sense to enjoy her food."

"That wasn't a fair test; I missed my supper last night."

"Just the same, I could see that you treated good

food with the proper respect," Ranger said. "Why don't you and me get us a cup of coffee down at Dave's—they have honest-to-God cream—and you can tell me what happened last night and get acquainted?"

He turned Ellen deftly toward the street, taking her consent for granted. "Be seeing you, boys. My appointment's at eleven, Doc."

As they walked away the elevator discharged Denise, devastating in halter and shorts on her way to the tennis courts. "Tom, darling! I didn't know you were here. Why haven't you come to see us?" She drew her red mouth into an adorable pout.

"Howdy, honey," Tom said easily, taking her hands. "You're beautiful as always. How's the rest of the family? Denise, do you know Miss Knowles?"

"We met last night." Denise nodded to Ellen. "When Susan got hit with a brick," she added, smiling.

"Were you in on that deal, too?" Tom asked. "We were going for some coffee, and Miss Knowles promised to tell me all about the excitement. Come with us?"

"No, thanks," Denise refused. "I never drink coffee, and my scales showed a pound too much this morning, so I must work that off. The baths reduce us some, but it's hard to stay just the right weight." Her glance flicked briefly at Ellen's contours. "Don't you think so, Miss Knowles?"

"I bet she's got more sense than to want to look like a stringbean," Tom said. "I watched her eat a dandy breakfast."

"Be careful, Miss Knowles!" Denise told her gaily. "It's easier to keep it off than to get it off!" She waggled the tennis racket at them and went out a side door.

"You don't need any off," Ranger said firmly, holding the door for Ellen.

Out of the corner of her eye Ellen inspected the man walking beside her. The result was impressive. He might have been carved from the southwestern cedar and titled a symphony in red and browns. Red-brown face, dark brown eyes, light brown hair sunburned to a crisp on the edges, the effect heightened by a cream gabardine shirt fitting snugly over a deep chest, and flawless frontier pants half revealing the remarkable boots. Ellen mentally tagged the flat-crowned felt hat at forty dollars and wished she had worn her best sport suit.

A gleam of the amusement she felt probably showed in her eyes as she looked up, for Ranger grinned and said, "Sure, I look like the heavy in a Grade B horse opera, but can't a man dress to please himself once in a while?"

Ellen laughed a little uncertainly, startled at the way he had read her thoughts.

Ranger went on earnestly, "Honest, back home in Dallas, you couldn't pick me outa the crowd to save your life—black shoes, blue serge, hard hat. But when I'm on vacation I express myself."

His face was completely serious, but the laugh wrinkles raying from his brown eyes deepened and the eyes themselves twinkled infectiously. Ellen laughed with him and surprised herself by saying:

"Don't tell a soul, but I'm dying to try one of those bare midriff things. So I admire you for being a man instead of a mouse."

"Why don't you get one?" Ranger asked. His eyes traveled over Ellen with obvious appreciation. "By golly, you'd look cute. Lots better than these little string beans that don't fill out—" His voice died away and his face grew red under its clear brown to match Ellen's fiery blush. They walked in silence for a moment. Then Ranger touched Ellen's arm.

"I hope I didn't offend you," he said in apology. "Ma raised me right, honest. Only I got a bad habit of knowing what I want and going right after it."

Ellen wondered what he meant by that, but aloud she told him that it was quite all right. Then she surprised herself again by thinking that she had really liked it!

Over Dave's coffee with the honest-to-God cream, she found the brown man more interesting by the minute.

"Ma wanted me to be a preacher," Ranger explained, "and Pop thought I ought to be a cattle buyer like him, so I fell between the two stools some way and turned out a policeman. But what I really want is to go to ranching. Do you like the country?" he asked abruptly.

"Of course," Ellen said.

"Now I'm not talking about country-at-the-edge-of-town; I mean forty-miles-to-the-next-neighbor country. Reckon you'd like that?"

"Yes, I think I would, although I don't see—"

Ranger nodded with satisfaction as if that settled something and leaped to another subject, with Ellen feeling like a muscle-bound mountain goat as she toiled at keeping up with him.

A few minutes before ten Ranger left her at the bath house door. As she went into the crowded lobby an elevator in the center discharged a cargo of house-coated women and others came down a stair that obviously connected with the hotel. Of course seriously ill people wouldn't be able to twist themselves in and out of street clothes to come in from the outside. She hadn't been very observant to miss seeing two elevator shafts and two stairways on each floor.

She looked about her curiously. Some of the bathers held tickets and so must have reservations; others crowded about the desk clerk hopefully. Ten o'clock must be a popular hour. There had been no one at all in the lobby yesterday afternoon when she had come in to start her series of baths.

Across the central hall from which the women's section opened, she could see men entering a similar room and being assigned bath numbers at an identical desk. The tall brown back turned to the desk clerk probably belonged to Ranger, for when he left her at the door he had remarked that while his baths wouldn't start until tomorrow after he had seen "Doc," he would step over and arrange for a favorite rubber.

"Good morning again, Miss Knowles," said a voice behind her. She turned to see Denise Chatham pushing a wheel chair from the elevators. The imperious little old lady sitting bolt upright in it was obviously Grandmother.

Her sharp black eyes scanned Ellen when the introductions were over. "I don't see anything the matter with you," she said abruptly. "You don't seem to belong here with the halt and the lame."

Denise answered for Ellen. "I bet she's a pushover for resort literature, Grandmother. Or maybe she believes in prevention instead of cure."

The old lady's drawn hands moved in her lap. "There isn't any cure, you know." Her voice was bleak. "But we have to do something."

The silence grew uncomfortable. Ellen glimpsed long years dominated by pain, relieved for a time by a new doctor with a new theory, a new treatment; of house aroused by serums, or electricity, or a high vitamin diet.

"I didn't know one could get down in that manner from the upper floors." Ellen nodded toward the elevator and stairs, feeling that her change of subject was clumsy.

"They're well hidden, so the porters can get more tips pointing them out." Denise went on then, seriously. "It's because they were put in after the hotel was built. The hotel, and the bath house too, have been remodeled, torn up, built over and added on to until nothing is what it seems. Halls turn into rooms, rooms turn into closets, windows and doors change places and stairs go backwards and sideways."

Old Mrs. Chatham looked severely at her granddaughter over her spectacles.

"That's only slightly exaggerated," Denise protested. "The new hotel and bath house down the street is far nicer and much more modern, but we've always come here. We're used to the queerness and we don't mind. And we think Doctor Doulton is a better doctor than the new man Fowler."

"No man who acts as Doctor Fowler does could be good at anything," old Mrs. Chatham said with a sniff. "When Doctor Campbell was alive and had the controlling interest in the old Thermal, there was the finest cooperation between the doctors. Now they don't even speak to each other. Childish. Like bolting the tunnel doors."

"Tunnels?" Ellen's curiosity made her ask, "Where?"

"See that door?" Denise pointed. "It's a tunnel that leads to the Thermal Bath Hall at the end of the block. A cross tunnel connects with the hotel across the street. Time was when people stayed at either hotel and took the baths wherever they pleased, but now if you stay here, you can't get a reservation for a series of baths over there to save your life. And if you go through the Doulton Clinic, they won't rent you a room at the Thermal."

"My wildest imagination wouldn't have put tunnels under these streets," Ellen marveled, "but I can see that they would be very convenient."

"Were, but aren't now. I don't know how useful they were to the grown-ups, but when we were kids Sandy and I played cops and robbers all over town and we certainly found them handy. We scrambled all over the hotel and bath house, inside and out, upstairs and down," Denise laughed.

"Late again," old Mrs. Chatham commented coldly, looking over Ellen's shoulder, her lips pressed tight in disapproval.

Coming toward them from the elevator, twisting a button into place and catching back a slipping hairpin, the housecoated woman was plainly the fourth Chatham. Once she too had had the family beauty, but pain had drawn her face and smudged dark shadows under the still beautiful eyes. The inexorable progress of her disease had pulled her head with its masses of heavy dark hair far to one side. This, with her odd hopping walk, gave her the pathetic look of a wounded bird. It was hard to look at Isobel Chatham casually.

When she had joined them and was hurriedly named to Ellen, Denise turned her grandmother's chair toward the baths. The old lady was in a pet about something, grumbling away as she was wheeled toward the desk, ringed with women getting bath numbers. Denise left the chair for a moment, turning back to Isobel and Ellen who were following more slowly as they talked.

"Grandmother says to go into the baths and tell Amy Lou to save Fourteen and Fifteen for you and for her. Amy Lou can tell whoever has the numbers there's been a mistake. Hurry, Isobel; she's sure you won't get them because you were late."

Without a word, Isobel accelerated her painful-looking, lurching walk and undertook the errand. Ellen wondered why Denise's brown young legs, shown to such advantage by the white shorts she wore, couldn't have gone to find the attendant.

Denise turned to Ellen and began, "It's one of life's more peculiar experiences, taking the baths in one of these small 'health' towns."

Ellen remembered what Susan had said. " 'Like living in a crazy twenty-one day microcosm,'" she quoted with a smile. "Susan said that in describing the little world of the hotels and the bath houses. Perhaps she exaggerated."

Denise shook her head, tossing the yellow curls off her forehead. "No, Sue always knows the right words and the longest ones for anything. If she called us a 'micro'—whatever you said, then that's it and—" She interrupted herself to look behind and upward with a startled face, then leap aside with a flash of long, perfect legs.

A whooping, play-suited child whizzed around the curve of the stair rail and landed on her feet. Her momentum sent her into a stumbling run that ended in Ellen's arms and backed them both staggering against Denise. Like stacked dominoes, all three sat down on the tiled floor. Denise reached out and seized the child and shook her till her black hair bound by a red ribbon flapped around her jeering face.

"You little rip!" she said between her teeth as the child twisted away from her. "I ought to—" Denise's violet eyes followed the sweep of the stair rail. "I'll bet you slid all the way from the third floor. It's a pity you didn't break your neck, Janie!"

"Boy, did I whizz! I souped it up with Mama's face cream!" The child ran away, on her small seat a greasy smear showing how she had attained the extra speed. Denise looked after her intently for a moment, then, laughing, sprang to her feet and extended a hand to Ellen.

"Never a dull moment! What did I tell you?"

Ellen drew a deep breath. "If the next nineteen days live up to the pace of the first two— I see what you mean."

Later, undressing in her booth, she saw Denise and the wheel chair stop before the last bath in the long row, and since Grandmother seemed mollified she supposed the bath was the desirable Fifteen. Desirable probably because it had more privacy, or it might have an outside window to circulate the steamy air.

Number Twelve could surely use some air cooling, she decided when the Egyptian of yesterday ushered her into her own tub. One day's experience had not accustomed her skin in the least to the steaming water. Ellen sweltered; she scorched; she sweat; she slowly parboiled as time, recorded by the indicator at the foot of the tub, stood still.

When five minutes had elapsed, the attendant appeared with a fresh cold towel and a cup of ice water, administered both and went on to the next bath without a word. Roused and refreshed by the coolness about her face, Ellen examined the bath compartment with more attention than she had yet given it. Sheets of grey marble shut her away from her neighbors on either side, the left hand wall reaching a height of about seven feet while the right hand wall against which the tub was placed looked nearly three feet higher. Probably the difference in height had something to do with the air circulation, she thought vaguely.

The compartments were arranged in pairs, then. No, she corrected the thought, they couldn't be in pairs and come out even, not with fifteen baths in the row. It didn't matter, except that she had a passion for making things come out even.

The tub, discolored about the faucets by the mineral waters, was outsize both in width and length. Ellen could just keep herself from floating upward by digging in with her toes while her head pressed back on the folded towel that served as a pillow. They ought to do something about that, she thought. There was no relaxation in it when you had to keep from bobbing like a cork. What did really short bathers do? And drowsy people must sometimes nod and dose, perhaps dipping their noses under the water for a startling instant. Surely the aged and the badly crippled must have some sort of device to hold them safely in the deep tubs. How did they manage old Mrs. Chatham, for instance?

As the indicator showed ten minutes of elapsed time, the attendant popped in again with a fresh towel and cup of water, punctual to the second. She asked, "Do you use soap, miss?" and not waiting for a reply, scoured Ellen vigorously before dashing out again.

"That's why she doesn't chatter," the surprised and

well soaped Ellen thought. "She doesn't have a second
to spare."

She adjusted her cool turban and settled down
flinchingly in the hot water to wait for the final minutes to pass. It was astonishing how quiet the bath
hall remained. She thought she heard a tiny popping
noise once or twice in Number Thirteen next door,
followed by a low murmur of some sort. Maybe the
water was running there. Number Thirteen could be
cheating by running some cold water in her bath.
Ellen wished she herself had thought to do that!

The prompt attendant did not appear when the last
five minutes had passed. After a little Ellen realized
that something had gone amiss. Out in the corridor,
beyond her vision, she heard an agitated voice and someone was told to "Run!" As she twisted around, trying
to see out of the doorway behind her, one of the bath
women ran past. From an opposite direction two
others hurried by, grey-faced and carrying one of the
rattan couches. Ellen leaned far over the edge of her
tub to reach her sheet and go see. Then the rubber
matting resounded to a running masculine tread and
Doctor Sandy, stethoscope in hand, crossed her line of
vision.

Ellen pulled the wet sheet around her and, shower-
ing water, went out of her compartment. A cluster of
people stood in front of Number Fifteen, nearly concealing the rattan couch. Over the increasing babble
of the bathers trying to find out what was wrong, she
heard Denise, her voice shrill and strange with fury.

"You shouldn't have let her start the baths, Sandy!

You should have known she was too old and weak! How much did you think her heart could stand? She wouldn't listen to me, but she would have given it up if you had told her. It's your fault she's dead! Yes, and Isobel's! And Amy Lou's! Isobel doesn't even know if the harness was broken when she fastened Grandmother in it. Amy Lou didn't even look at it."

Denise dropped her distorted face into her hands and began to sob. "Grandmother's drowned! Drowned! Because of you, all three!"

CHAPTER V

It was cool on the side porch at Susan's. Ellen took off her hat and thought wistfully about kicking off her pumps, but decided against it. She leaned back in the reed chair and closed her eyes. Brown Sugar, watching for Susan to reappear through the house door, flattened herself like a frog against the cool tiles and panted mightily.

It had been insufferably hot in the church and scarcely less so at the cemetery where old Mrs. Chatham had been buried in the family plot, melancholy with spruce and cedar. A little group of old friends from the town and the hotel, a larger number of acquaintances like Ellen herself, and a crowd of the curious had stood under the stifling shade of the undertaker's tent. Just such a group had listened earlier when the coroner pronounced the death accidental drowning.

When the gate clicked Ellen opened her eyes to see Sandy and Tom Ranger walking between the rows of wilted balsam and petunias. They lowered themselves into chairs, but nobody said much even when Susan came back with a tray of drinks. "Grandmother went to lie down," she said. "This has been hard on her. She and Miss Sara were girls together."

The level in his glass had been reduced two-thirds before Sandy stretched his legs and sighed. "Well, Dad and I took them back to the hotel, and they've decided to stay until Isobel and Charles finish their course of baths. I didn't know I would feel so grateful."

"Their staying on should help," Ellen said.

"Looks like it would."

"Felt it already, I reckon?" Tom's brows crooked inquiringly.

"I had three people during my office hours this morning, and twenty guests have checked out at the hotel. I haven't checked the bath house, but I'll bet nobody's had a bath for three days."

Ellen was indignant. "I've gone right on with mine every day."

Sandy smiled a little. "You and Tom and maybe a few more hardy souls."

"I thought Denise seemed a little better today, didn't you?" Susan moved to sit on the stool by Sandy's feet, her brown eyes as anxious as those of the small dog.

"At least she no longer blames me exclusively." Sandy had a wry look on his face. "At first it was every bit my fault for letting old Miss Sara even think about baths at her age and in her condition. I kept telling Denise that the old lady's heart was as sound as a winter apple with every indication of going strong for several more years. But she kept saying I should have known better."

"That a fact, Sandy?" Ranger asked with interest.

"The old lady's heart was good?"

"It sounded all right to me." Sandy was silent a moment, and then retreated from his positive statement with medical caution. "Anybody knows the heart is an unpredictable organ. People who have never had a single warning have one severe attack and die of it. And it's become a common saying that the way to live to be a hundred is to find out early that you have a bad heart. But old Miss Sara didn't die from heart failure except in the sense that every death is that essentially. She drowned. She might have had some pain or a sinking spell that made her drop against the safety strap and break it, but she definitely drowned."

"But you're damned if she did and damned if she didn't," Ranger said flatly. "According to the public, you either made a fatal mistake as a doctor or your bath house is run with criminal carelessness."

"You can say that again." Sandy's voice was bitter. "Somebody should have noticed the safety strap was worn. Old Miss didn't weigh a hundred pounds."

Susan caught the hands he had slapped down on his knees and held them tightly, her brown eyes wide and deep with sympathy. "Denise shouldn't blame you," she said. "Something that no one could foresee —isn't that what they call an act of God? Old Miss Sara couldn't have lived much longer anyway. And I don't think she thought so, either," Susan concluded surprisingly.

"You mean she thought she was going to die?" Tom asked.

Susan nodded. "The night they were here for supper she kept saying that she had to get her affairs in order; that she didn't have much time left."

Ellen shrugged. "Surely that's a natural thought when you've reached eighty-seven."

"Not for Miss Sara, it wasn't. She always planned like she was going to live forever. Once Grandmother and I went to see her when they still lived here. It was her seventy-fifth birthday and guess what she was doing? Planting white pine seeds! She'd decided to replace the avenue of oaks with pine trees."

"She figgered on ninety-five at least, if she intended to see those pines get sizeable," Tom said thoughtfully. "And barring accidents, I reckon she'd have made it, too. She was a determined old woman."

"And domineering," Sandy added. "Iron hand in black lace mitts. I used to wonder why Charles or Isobel or Denise didn't defy her, but then they'd never had any practice planning anything for themselves, let alone a rebellion."

"They were really devoted to her, Sandy," Susan protested. "The night they were here, every time old Miss Sara said anything about not having time left Charles and Isobel looked so distressed, and Denise even had tears in her eyes. One time Denise ran to her grandmother and threw her arms around her neck," Susan recalled, "and she said, 'Oh, darling, don't talk like that! You know very well you have your hundredth birthday party planned to the last detail!' "

"And what did Miss Sara say to that?" Tom asked.

"She sat up stiff as a ramrod and snapped, 'Plans! I'm still perfectly able to change my plans or make new ones!' "

"Now what did she mean by that?" Tom wondered.

"We all laughed when Denise told her, 'Now, Grandmother, that's carrying independence too far to trade off a birthday party for a funeral! And just to prove that you can change your plans.' And then Denise kissed her and said. "And don't bark at me, darling. Barking grannies never bite.' "

"Old Miss Sara didn't laugh with us, though," Susan went on. "She shrugged Denise away, and her voice was still sharp when she said, 'There's one bite in every dog and every grannie.' "

"That was a curious conversation," Sandy said. "But old Miss Sara liked to be obscure and mysterious about everything. Hollis Sears is her lawyer, and he's got stomach ulcers over her business affairs. She never let her right hand know what her left hand was doing, not to mention her lawyer."

There was a silence on the cool porch for a time, broken only by the musical clinkings of ice and the drone of bees in the rows of balsam. Ellen noted that Sandy still held the hands that had comforted him and that the furrows in his forehead had smoothed out a little.

Tom Ranger caught Ellen's eye and motioned to the door. He emptied the ice from his glass into a flower pot and looked at his watch.

"Quarter to seven," he announced. "Well, be seein' you. We're going to catch a bite to eat."

At La Posta, as Ellen explored her enchilada with a fascinated fork, Ranger went back to the accident. She thought with resignation that she hadn't heard about anything else for three days.

"Let's see, you saw them in front of Number Fifteen. Denise doesn't see Grandmother into her bath personally as she usually does because she has a headache and goes out to the desk to get an aspirin. But she asks Isobel to be sure that Grandmother is all right and Isobel does, so she says."

Tom stopped to ask her, "What did you say? Don't mutter at me."

"Mutter dear!" Ellen enunciated snappishly. "I said Isobel always does, doesn't she?"

Tom gave her a puzzled glance, but returned to his summary. "Then Denise comes back, looks in and asks, 'How are you, darling?' and gets into her own bath. I wonder why she takes them anyway?" Tom interrupted himself to ask. "Amy Lou goes in when the five minutes is up, and Grandmother is fine. When Amy Lou comes back in another five minutes Grandmother is still O.K. But when she cames back again, the old lady is out of the broken safety strap and floating in the tub. They take her out of the water and send for Sandy, but it's too late. All Sandy can say about the strap is that they put new ones in every season in case the water weakens them. Nobody remembers looking at the strap special for some time. Isobel says she did, but not at the webbing, just at the buckle to be sure it was fastened. The girls are naturally upset; Denise especially saying a lot of things she probably doesn't mean and blaming everybody."

Ellen interrupted the soliloquy. "When did the Chathams live here? I was surprised to hear that this town was once their home."

"Have you seen that big red brick with the pillars on the hill out in town? They lived there, and while the old gentleman was alive—Miss Sara's husband— they had more money than you could shake a stick at. The old gentlemen was a doctor and so was Denis Chatham, Denise's father. Something happened—I never heard just what—and they left here and went to Georgia to live on a plantation they own there. So it's natural they would come back here when they need the baths, I reckon they've spent a fortune on doctors and treatments for the three of them. I don't suppose they have much left now."

Ellen said nothing, and Ranger, too, ate in silence for a while. Then he sat back in his chair and scrubbed his chin with his knuckles in a thoughtful manner. She waited, but he continued to say nothing.

"What is it?" she asked. "What have you thought of now?"

"Nothing new. I keep wondering how the old lady got that bump on the back of her head. Seems she would've slid forward when the strap broke, don't it?"

Of course it was the enchilada. She should have remembered that her stomach wasn't so receptive to exotic foods as it might once have been. And along

with the indigestion she was too hot. If she opened
the louvers of the door that might set up a better
circulation of air.

Back in her bed again, it did seem cooler. She lay
looking at the pattern of black bars the opened slats
made on the floor. The moon must be shining brightly
through the hall window to make it so distinct. She
began to feel drowsy. Vaguely she noticed that the
moonlight flickered and half of the patterned bars disappeared. Again the moonlight flickered and the bars
of shadow showed again on the floor.

Then eyes and brain coordinated so sharply that she
gasped. Moonlight didn't flicker! There was someone
in the hall; someone who had stood silently at her
door to block out the moonlight. Ellen sat up indignantly, then swung her feet to the floor. She would
see who went peeping in the middle of the night.

Listening a moment before she carefully turned the
latch and then the door knob so that she made no
sound, she heard nothing. Then she opened the door
an inch and peered out into the hall. Where she stood
the moonlight streamed from a window in the end of
the ell, but both ends of the hall were in shadow. Over
the elevator doors a red globe burned dimly; at the
other end over the stairs the white sign, "To the
Baths," glimmered faintly. There was nothing else.
Whoever had looked or listened at her door had
moved fast. Or maybe she had dreamed it.

She cast a look at the empty hall and turned to go
back to bed. Then she heard it: the faintest noise that

told her she had not been dreaming. There was someone in the hall, out of sight somewhere; someone who
was anxious not to be seen. More puzzled than ever,
Ellen silently closed her door, sure now that someone watched. Then she stood inside her room listening
with all the power of her very sharp ears.

After what seemed like hours she heard again the
tiny protest of a trodden board. Not a careful, cautious step in the hall; the sound was not quite right
for that. She waited again, but the sound was not repeated. She was no doubt making a very large mountain out of a very small molehill. What if some late
guest had passed her door? Maybe he had had the
same reaction to her opening door that she had had
to his passing! Ellen smiled a little and told herself,
We're a pair of fools together.

Then memory identified the sound. Nothing made
that indescribable creaking whisper but a stair tread.
What on earth was anyone doing on the stairs lead-
ing to the baths at this time of night? So full of curiosity that caution found no room, Ellen belted her
robe around her and let herself out.

When she reached the shadowy end of the hall
she crept silently to look over the banisters, but whoever was on the stairs had reached the landing turn
and was out of sight from above. She heard nothing
and saw nothing. As she started down on the stairs
she put into practice a bit of knowledge that her passion for old houses had taught her. Old stairs creaked
because the nails in the tread had loosened, but the

oldest and creakiest seldom made a sound if you followed them down close to the wall.

No light from the small globe over the stair head reached beyond the landing turn. Ellen stood there a long time getting up her courage to descend the well of darkness that was the second flight. At last, carefully shifting her weight from one foot to the next, she went down, stopping often to listen. But the silence was as palpable as the darkness.

Then as she felt for the next step, suddenly she was afraid. Her curiosity was gone, leaving in its place a growing panic that made it physically impossible to take another step forward into the darkness. Whoever had gone down the stairs might not welcome a companion on his secret journey.

She turned around and started back up, her relief growing at every tread. What had she been thinking about to start on such a harebrained journey in the first place? The landing was only a few steps higher and her room and safety only a few feet away. Her outstretched hand felt along the inside wall so that she could climb as close to it as possible. The rough feel of the plaster was somehow reassuring. She felt something smooth; of course, the strip of wood that protected the plaster corner at the landing. Then with a terror that froze her, her fingertips recognized not wood but stiffly starched cloth!

How long she stood there with her hand touching that motionless arm Ellen never knew. She literally couldn't move to save her life. A scream began to grow in her throat, and she waited for the throttling hands that would silence it. But the hands, surprisingly, did not choke her. Instead they pushed violently and she felt herself falling backward, down the stairs.

CHAPTER VI

Ellen hurriedly pushed the hand mirror under her pillow as she heard the knock at her door. She considered that she looked very well in the blue bed jacket Susan had sent. Her bruises, if still painful, were not in visible places.

"Come in," she called. It was her first day for visitors and she found that she was looking forward to company. Two days of her own exclusive society were more than enough.

It was Sandy with Isobel Chatham. "I met her in the hall and brought her along," he explained. "But naturally the rescuer wants to know how the rescued is making out." He noticed the look of surprise on Ellen's face. "Didn't I tell you it was Isobel who heard your crash landing and found you unconscious?"

"You certainly didn't. Every time I've opened my mouth you either put a thermometer in it or told me not to talk while you made like the Sphinx."

"You were really very fortunate," Isobel said. "When I found you I thought—" her voice broke, but she resumed, "it was another fatal accident."

Ellen looked the sympathy she felt. She answered

slowly, "I'm surprised myself that it wasn't fatal. But it was no accident."

The astonishment on the two faces was gratifying. "I was pushed," Ellen said indignantly.

Sandy hooted at the idea. "On the back stairs? Who could have pushed you? Why should anybody push you? You must have slipped, Ellen." He was final. "I looked at your slipper soles myself and they're as slick—what do you do, wax them?—and it was plain to see where the rubber heel made a black mark on the edge of a tread. You saw it, didn't you, Isobel?"

Isobel nodded. "That is true about the mark on the step, but I did wonder what you were doing on the stairs at that time of night."

"I wasn't the only one on the stairs," Ellen said. She told how she had tried to discover who had passed and paused at her door, then gone down the stairs to the baths. She could see that they were having trouble believing her, and even to her own ears the story sounded fantastic.

When she had finished Sandy said, "Slipped or pushed, only that lazy porter saved you from broken bones or worse. Isobel found you in the laundry hampers at the foot of the stairs, mixed up in the wet towels. If Witless had put the laundry in the back entry as he's supposed to do—" He shrugged his shoulders.

"Could it have been Witless or one of the other elevator boys?" Isobel was thoughtful. With her lurching walk she went to the small table near the door and picked up a package. As she stripped off the green waxed tissue, she said to Ellen in the offhand manner of the shy, "I made it for you. I hope you'll like it."

The shallow amber glass bowl held a miniature desert scene, perfect in every detail. The tiny plants among the rocks and sand dunes were so carefully scaled that they gave an illusion of depth and distance to the little garden. Ellen was charmed and said so.

"Where did you get so many tiny plants?" she asked. "And all growing, too."

"I collect them and keep them growing in some window boxes. I have some of those small paraffined paper ones that I keep with me. In a hotel miniature gardens are all I can manage. I always start a group of plants for Dora Martingale to use as decoratives when I come, of course, so I don't get too lonesome for my garden at home." Isobel talked with the animation of the hobby rider. "But these tiny things are fun. Finding them is just the beginning. Then you have the same problems of soil and drainage, spraying and dusting for insects and diseases that you have with the largest shrubs."

"Aren't most of these wild plants?"

"I get them in fields and along roadsides." Isobel nodded. She looked at Ellen with a faint smile. "This ungainly gait of mine is more painful to the onlookers than to me. I walk a great deal."

While Ellen searched for something to say, Sandy crossed the room to answer a knock at the door. "This will let me out," he told Ellen. "You can get up any time now. Take it easy and no bath until tomorrow." With one motion he opened the door for Dora Martingale, twiddled his fingers in a gesture of farewell and was gone.

When the door finally closed behind the woman, Ellen took a deep breath and leaned back on her pillows. She was beginning to feel hungry when she was startled by an explosive knock at the door, but it proved to be Ranger instead of her supper tray. Her caller bristled visibly, and his Stetson was pushed to the back of his head at an angle of exasperation.

"Forty-five blasted minutes!" he fumed. "Stuck in that—that—" He couldn't find a qualifying adjective both adequate and fit for a lady's ears. "Elevator between the second and third floors with five screechin' women. Forty-five minutes! Damned if I don't think that rattlin' female's right; whole place is goin' to hell in a handbasket!"

Ellen giggled. Ranger looked at her ominously for a moment and then a grin began to replace the frown. He threw his hat into a chair and, sitting down on the edge of the bed, took her hand.

"I was so mad I forgot my manners," he said. "How are you, Ellen? I've been plenty worried about you. Why, you fool girl, it's a wonder you didn't kill yourself."

Ellen found that she liked being called a girl, even prefaced by such an unflattering adjective. She felt herself going pink and so answered tartly, "I might have been killed all right, but I didn't do it myself. And go sit in a chair, Tom Ranger, or I won't have a shred of reputation left."

Ranger looked at her seriously. "What do you mean, you didn't do it yourself?"

Ellen told him about her terror on the stairs and the horrible starched arms. And she could see that Ranger, bless him, believed her. When she finished he said nothing for a moment. Ellen grew conscious that both her hands were being held reassuringly tight and pulled away from his grasp. Tom did not seem to notice and continued to whistle softly between his teeth.

"Something very peculiar goes on around here," he said at last. Reaching into a shirt pocket, he brought out a small object and handed it to her. "Do you know anything about that?"

Ellen turned it over in her hands. It was an ordinary pearl button of the type removable for laundering. She shook her head.

"It was in your hand when we put you to bed," Tom said. "That pin thing on the back was caught in the band of your ring. Seemed likely you'd got tangled up with it in the laundry hamper, but from force of habit I sorted through all of it and there wasn't a solitary other button like it on anything."

"Then where did it come from? I certainly didn't have it in my hand when I started."

"I went around to the laundries and looked at the clean stuff going out, and here's something else peculiar. That button is like the others on Doctor Fowler's fancy office coats. And while I was there his secretary called up and raised the devil about the laundry breaking the buttons off last week's wash."

Ellen frowned. "Where would Doctor Fowler fit in?"

Tom shrugged. "I don't know. Shouldn't think he'd push a good-looking woman downstairs. He'd be more likely to—" Tom let the sentence trail away.

Ellen traced the pattern of tufting on the bedspread with a preoccupied finger. She felt that the conversation would benefit by a change of subject. "I'm sure it was some kind of uniform; there was that smooth starchy feel nothing else has." Her mouth fell open a little as a thought struck her. "Tom! It could have been that nurse!"

"What nurse?"

"I've forgotten her name, but Dora Martingale said she used to be head nurse at the Clinic, and she's plainly queer. She called Hampton Potts a bumble bee and illustrated how he buzzed by making circles around her head."

Tom nodded. "You mean Liz Elliott. Sure, she's a little off her rocker, but she's harmless."

"It's not harmless to push people downstairs in the middle of the night," Ellen objected.

"You don't know it was her."

"I don't know it was anybody, but the black and blue spots on my—well, I certainly didn't imagine them!" Ellen said hotly.

"Of course you didn't, sugar," Tom soothed. "I only meant I doubted that it was Loony Liz because I think there's some plan in this funny stuff. Only I don't see what it could be."

"That makes it seem surer that some crazy person's

up to crazy tricks."

"Could be, but I don't cotton to the notion some-how."

Around the edge of the half open door Ellen saw a movement, then a red hair ribbon, and two sharp eyes regarded them from a point about four feet from the floor.

"Ain't canoodling," said a disappointed mutter.

Tom turned his head following Ellen's eyes. "You shoulda seem us a while ago," he said. Then his twinkle deepened, but his face assumed a stern look. "Janie Jeris, you come in here," he commanded. "Usual type of hotel hellion," he added to Ellen.

The red hair ribbon and the sharp black eyes be-longed to the small girl of the stair rail sliding episode. She looked pertly and with adult understanding at the two of them and remarked, "Mama said you'd been in here for a long time and *she* said *she* couldn't think what you were doing!"

"We were minding out own business, which is more than your Mama was," Tom snapped. He stood up somewhat hastily from the side of the bed and sat down again in the platform rocker. "What are you doing snooping indoors on a fine day like this, Janie? Why don't you go outside and play?"

"I am not snooping," Janie retorted. "Besides, there nothing else to do. A piece is lost off my new skates, and there's nobody to play with." The pertness of her manner slipped and Ellen saw underneath, a lonely child living in an adult world.

"It's dull for you here, isn't it, Janie?" she asked

sympathetically. "I tell you, you and I will have a picnic. I'm tired of staying indoors, too."

"Could we cook our supper?" Janie asked eagerly.

"I don't know why not," Tom said. "I'll get some steaks and show you how to barbecue over coals."

"Does he hafta come?" Janie asked bluntly.

Ellen looked at Tom and laughed, but before she could answer the child's question, Tom said earnestly, "Pretty please, Janie. You're not the only one who's got nobody to play with."

CHAPTER VII

Next morning Ellen joined the veranda coterie for the first time. She dreaded the chatter, but the prospect of a fine morning spent inside the four walls of her room was not alluring. She still creaked like a rusty hinge as she went down the hall after a leisurely breakfast in bed and a bath that she had managed for herself, but she was too glad to be out again to mind.

"How nice to see you out, Miss Knowles," said the sirupy voice of Mrs. Jeris. Sharp black eyes like Janie's flicked over Ellen from head to foot with the beady impersonal look of a bird. Her smooth, glossy head cocked slightly on a short neck added to the illusion which she completed by speaking with a kind of darting peck. "We've been so concerned about you. Absolutely everyone. Of course that nice Mr. Ranger was nearly distracted." Her voice was arch, and Ellen could feel herself turning red.

"Everyone's been awfully kind," she murmured.

On their way to open the library, Susan and Brown Sugar stopped to leave a book for Ellen and, seeing her on the veranda, delivered it on the spot. Susan's merry red mouth drooped a bit at the corners, but she spoke gayly enough.

"You're trespassing. This corner is reserved for Mr. Charles so he can enjoy the morning minus the matrons!" Her voice became serious. Sure you're all right, Ellen? We've been worried."

At the anxious note in her mistress' voice, Sugar's mournful spaniel face grew longer. She laid her chin on Ellen's knee and with great dignity wagged her feathered stern.

"Of course," Ellen made her voice cheerful and brisk. "But if I wasn't, I wouldn't say so. I've had enough audible sympathy. Dumb animals are better at it."

Susan laughed and Sugar accelerated the tail wagging. Lowering her eyes, the girl pulled small green leaves from the vine beside her, dropping them for the dog to leap at. "I'm scared," she confessed. "Not that anything will happen to me, for I don't see where I could fit into the picture at all. But something very queer is going on."

Ellen was startled at the repetition; that was what Tom had said.

"There's a plan behind this monkey business," Susan went on. "Sandy says I read too many whodunits." She looked up at Ellen then with fear in her brown eyes. "Maybe you do fit in, Ellen. Be awfully careful, won't you? Maybe this isn't the end of it."

"I've heard bad luck comes in threes; mine should be the last accident." Ellen looked at the girl intently dropping leaves for the spaniel to catch. "Sandy can take it," she told her gently.

"He's a fighter, but you can't fight this," Susan said fiercely. "It's like trying to land a good punch in a barrel of molasses!" She made a face at her watch and ran off down the path, the spaniel at her heels.

Ellen was alone only a few moments. Before she could collect her thoughts, Charles Chatham propelled his wheel chair around the corner and looked nonplussed to find his usual place occupied. On an impulse Ellen insisted that there was plenty of room for him and told him brightly and falsely that she was just going up to her room in any case.

While she searched around in her mind for a suitable opening gambit, the man startled her by asking, "What do you want to talk to me about?"

She looked up in surprise to meet his amused gaze. "I have been a lawyer, Miss Ellen, and a certain facility at mind reading is often found in those who successfully practice." With a faint smile, he added, "At one time I was considered the best lawyer in Georgia."

Ellen leaned back in her chair and laughed. Then, becoming serious, she asked him, "What do you make of these extraordinary accidents?" Too late, she realized she was asking the man to talk about his own mother's death.

Charles Chatham did not seem to find it a strange question. Tossing his silver hair back into place, he looked at Ellen somberly. "That they are not accidental, but parts of a careful and ingenious plan."

For a moment she blinked at him. This was more than she expected, but she realized that she had been pushing her reluctant mind to the same conclusion.

"Mind you," the man went on, "I don't think the accidents have turned out altogether as planned." He sat in silence for a time. "I loved my mother, Miss Ellen, and I believe she could have expected several more years of life. Now I say to you, and very shortly I am going to say the same thing to the proper authorities, that whoever caused her to drown is going to pay for her death.

"To be as physically inactive as I am gives one time to think and opportunity to observe," the man continued soberly. "From those thoughts and observations I have a kind of patchwork, piecing together the whole picture of motives and actions. I need only a piece or two more; then the picture will be complete and—" he paused, then added, "incriminating."

He was almost talking to himself, Ellen thought. She felt sure he had forgotten her.

"Imagine a boulder on a mountainside," he went on. "Left alone in its imbedded place, it is at worst a nuisance to be climbed over or walked around, but it is not a menace. Pried loose, it crashes to destroy everything in its pathway and dashes itself to pieces at the last. Self-love is like that. Imbedded in a character, it is an ugly thing. Moved by the levers of ambition, jealousy, greed, or fear, it becomes a force of evil destroying the innocent and the guilty alike."

The man's eyes lost their far away look and he smiled wryly at Ellen. "There you are. My observations are either profound psychological truths or the subconscious voice of a dyspeptic stomach!" With his face falling into strained, serious lines, he added as if everything should be clear to her now. "And that's the explanation of this series of pseudo-accidents."

He held up a finger to silence any reply she might have made, then with another change of subject that left the already floundering Ellen still farther behind, he spoke in a bantering tone.

"You really don't belong here, you know. Ladies come to rest and get slim by taking the baths. You obviously don't need slimming, and you must not need rest or you wouldn't have the energy to fall down stairs in the middle of the night."

"Oh, here you are, all cozy with Uncle Charles!" a gay voice interrupted. Ellen mentally gave Charles Chatham one for sharp ears; she hadn't heard anyone approaching. Coming around the corner, Denise looked cool and beautiful in a blue dress that covered more than usual of her lovely figure. She carried a large tray. "I've been looking for you upstairs, Miss Ellen. Look what I have for you."

Ellen looked at the home-made candy arranged so temptingly. "How nice." She smiled her thanks. "You must have known every tooth I have is a sweet one. Um, two kinds of fudge!"

"Try this one first." Denise turned the tray and pointed. "I'd like to know what you think of it. Sour cream and orange rind; my own invention. Uncle Charles, here's some of the only kind you ever eat. Isobel was in the kitchen, too, making goodnight fruit, so I put some slices of it on the tray."

"What in the world is 'goodnight fruit?'" Ellen asked.

Denise pointed out some disks looking rather like fruit cake. "It's health candy: raisins, prunes, figs and apricots chopped up with lemon juice. No one actually needs it here while we drink these nasty waters, but it's habit with us and distressingly good for one."

"I'll try some of it later on, but now, since Mr. Charles assures me I needn't worry about my figure, I'll concentrate on the fudge. It's marvelous."

"Denise is an accomplished cook," said her uncle. "She can even make the diet for peptic ulcers interesting. In fact, now that I seriously consider it, everything she does is very well done indeed." He nibbled at the fruit candy in his hand. "I doubt that we've quite appreciated her abilities."

"Go on, Uncle Charles, you say that to all the girls!" Denise laughed as she sat down on the edge of the porch. "I'll never amount to a hill of beans; I'm too lazy."

"I believe that's right, too," the man said reflectively. "Well, you must excuse me, ladies; I'm a ten o'clock bather." He maneuvered his chair, turning expertly down the short ramp that led from the porch to a sidewalk.

Across the lawn, Sandy with his hands deep in the pockets of his white jacket walked slowly toward the Clinic. He looked up and smiled briefly when Denise called to him, then stood kicking the gravel in the path until she joined him. The eight o'clock bathers were coming out of the bath house. Instead of the small crowds of a week ago, they were emerging by ones and twos. Ellen counted rapidly. Six men and five women, when the baths were normally filled to capacity at the height of the season. No wonder Sandy's shoulders had lost their usual cocky brace.

Ranger emerged and stood mopping his face and talking earnestly with a man she had not seen among the guests. He turned to lean against the wall with a foot braced on a tubbed oleander and caught sight of Ellen half hidden in the viny corner. He brought his conversation to an end and walked across the grass to the porch. He sat down and, unbuttoning a cuff of the gabardine shirt, pushed up the sleeve.

"Looky," he invited briefly.

"What on earth?" Ellen made little clucking sounds. The muscular forearm was painfully red and looked badly burned.

Tom rolled down the sleeve before he answered. "I swear I've scalded hogs in water that wasn't that hot! Something went haywire with the thermostat and three, four of us got pretty well cooked. You know how they pour water over the aching spot? The bath boys take it out of a special tank so it won't be too hot, but man alive, it was fire this morning!"

Tom's voice was harsh. "A few of the crazy things happening around here could be accidents, but not all."

Ellen remembered, "Charles Chatham wants to have a talk with you. He doesn't think it's all accidents, either."

"He doesn't?" Tom asked with interest. "What did he say?"

"I hardly know," Ellen said slowly. "He was really

disturbed, but most of the time I couldn't follow him. He talked about self-love and jealousy, and greed, and fear—and something about a boulder on a mountainside."

"He got four of the strongest motives, when he names those." Tom got up and picked up his hat. "Aren't you a ten o'clocker? Come on then; it's time."

He gave her a hand to pull her up from the deck chair and they walked toward the bath house. At the door he stopped and held her back with a hand on her arm.

"Look, Ellen, you keep your eyes open and be careful. I'm going to get busy. That was the sheriff I was talking to a while ago—it's the Lord's mercy the Chief of Police is taking his vacation; you couldn't find a bigger clabberhead in a day's travel. Nobody's going to push my girl downstairs and scald me like a hog for butcherin'!"

Ellen stared after his stiffly held back.

CHAPTER VIII

Tom whistled a two-toned accolade of admiration. "Ellen, honey, you're prettier than a Jersey heifer!"

Ellen thought she ought to be. The yellow pique dress had cost more than two weeks salary, and the hairdresser's hodge podge of curls had been three dollars more and a total loss, for she had washed them out and achieved the coronet of braids that added an illusory inch to her height herself.

"By golly, I sure made a good guess," Tom went on with satisfaction, holding out a transparent box of crisp yellow daisies. "Want me to pin 'em on?"

Ellen backed away from his eagerness in some alarm, thinking that the girl who had sold her the perfume must have been right about its seductiveness. "I think I'll tuck them in my hair," she decided, turning to the mirror. "They're lovely, Tom, and my favorites."

"Sure enough? I thought they looked kinda like you." Tom's eyes met hers in the glass and Ellen turned away in slight confusion to pick up her bag and handkerchief.

He grinned down at her. "Let's go. You look good

enough to eat, but I'm saving up for baked ham and spoon bread."

Susan's grandmother had asked them to supper and persuaded the three Chathams to come. With the Doultons, the list concluded well within the bounds old Mrs. Beauregard considered correct for a recently bereaved family.

"How will Mr. Charles get there?" Ellen asked.

"He hired Witless, the elevator boy, to push his wheel chair. Charles rambles around considerable of evenings. He doesn't like being stared at daytimes."

Charles, Isobel and Denise sat talking with old Mrs. Beauregard and Susan as they came in, and the two Doultons soon followed. Then on the elder doctor's arm, the white-haired hostess led them into the dining room.

As Sandy pushed Denise's chair in, she smiled over her shoulder at him. "Do you remember the time I bribed you with a whole week's allowance to pull the chair out just a little? The time we had Miss Hawsey to dinner?"

Sandy laughed. "My mother saw it and fined me two weeks allowance. That was when I learned that Crime Does Not Pay."

"Grandmother guessed I had planned it and she kept me penniless for a month." Denise laughed a little wryly. "Not that being a pauper was anything unusual."

Charles Chatham looked at her with level eyes. "You had everything you needed, Denise."

"Yes, I suppose I did," Denise agreed. "But the distance between 'need' and 'want' is so great!"

"Mother was always careful to see that we lacked for nothing," Isobel entered the conversation. "She planned everything so our lives ran along as smoothly as possible. She was a wonderful manager."

"To put it a little more bluntly," Denise said, her violet eyes sharp with malice, "she drove Grandfather and my father and you and Uncle Charles like a four-in-hand. I was the colt, expected to follow close or feel the whip!"

"Denise!" Isobel said in a shocked voice.

Denise was contrite. "Forgive me, darlings. You know my tongue always runs away with me. I reckon it's that low Yankee blood I got from my mother."

Old Matilde Beauregard interposed calmly, "I used to tell Sara you need more discipline than you ever got, Denise. You know very well you wound the whole household around your fingers. You always had your own way. You were a stubborn, spoiled, head-strong child!"

"And all the time I thought no one had caught onto my little tricks!"

Everyone laughed then and the conversation turned to general topics.

As they drove home down the hill, later, the head-lights picked up Charles Chatham, his dramatic shock of hair argent in the moonlight, propelled along by the shambling Witless. Tom turned away from the hotel at the end of the street and drove down quiet country lanes, sleeping under the moon. After a half-hour he brought them back to the Eureka where they all went up to their rooms with no more than a murmured goodnight.

Ellen had been standing at her window for some time looking out at the climbing moon when a dark object hurtled down from above to crash to the ground. A frightened, intermittent yelling rose and fell like a siren. Fear rose in a choking flood in Ellen's throat, but she found herself running up the stairs to the third floor as doors flew open and lights clicked on.

Witless, his face gray and loose with terror, clutched at Tom's arms. "Mista Cha'les! Mista Cha'les went fallin' off that balcony!"

Tom shook off the man's hands and ran into Charles Chatham's room. The hair on Ellen's head really rose in terror when she heard Charles' resonant, panting voice through the thud of Tom's strides.

Above Witless' wailing, the voice said, "Don't come out here. The balcony might not hold us both. Get a chair and I'll try to catch it."

Seconds later, Tom picked up the wasted body that he had pulled from the balcony railing clinging to the chair. "Turn the bed down, Ellen," he said with no surprise at her presence. "Witless, stop that caterwauling and get Sandy."

Charles spoke with difficulty. "I don't think I'm hurt beyond bruises. I always—" his pajamaed chest rose and fell with his panting breath—"go to the windows before I call Witless to get me into bed. The chair simply shot out." His eyes, dilated with shock, stared into the shadowy corner. "I threw myself sideways. Just in time."

His eyes closed wearily as the door into the con-
necting room flew open and Isobel hurried to her
brother. Denise followed, tying a robe that clung to
her wet body.

CHAPTER IX

The womens' lobby was empty. Looking at the clock, Ellen saw that she was a few minutes late, but no doubt there were plenty of baths unoccupied. The hotel seethed with rumors and surmises over Charles Chatham's narrow escape of the night before, and probably most of the regulars were exchanging the latest. Busy with her own thoughts, she left her clothes in the dressing stalls and emerged in the tan sheet that was the bathers' uniform.

Halfway down the row of baths, Bella, the rubber, beckoned to her. Ellen padded in, in her flappy paper slippers, and noticing that it was Number Eight, asked on a sudden impulse if Number Fifteen was in use.

Bella shook her head. "No, ma'am, it hasn't been used since the day of the accident. You mean you want to use that bath?" She shrugged her thin shoulders and, muttering something that sounded like, "No, not if you paid me! No, ma'am!" she led Ellen down to the end of the row.

Stripped of her sheet and in the tub of water—which she had tested carefully before stepping in—Ellen wondered herself why she was there. Maybe she was the morbid type! She braced her toes at the end of the tub and thought about the plague of accidents that beset the Eureka. At any rate it took part of her mind away from thinking how infernally hot she was.

Wiping her streaming face, she wondered if the thermostat was really working. When Bella popped in, she asked her if the water wasn't hotter than usual.

Bella wound a cold towel around Ellen's head before she answered. "You can see for yoreself, miss; the pointer's smack on a hundred. You're just not used to it yet."

Ellen muttered that she never expected to get used to being boiled alive.

Bella grinned and bobbed her head toward the corner of the compartment. "Since you like this stall, you ought to take one of the fizzy baths; they're not hot."

Ellen was amazed. "Do you mean there's a way to take these baths without boiling like a pot full of shrimp?" she demanded. "And why hasn't someone told me about it before now?"

"I don't rightly think Doctor Sandy would've prescribed them for you, miss. They're just for the old and the feeble."

"How is it done, Bella?"

The black woman indicated the corner again. Ellen had noticed the machine there and wondered what it was. She had seen nothing like it in any of the other compartments in which she had bathed.

"I don't rightly know myself," Bella said. "I never

gave any of 'em. Not very often I work in the baths. I think you turn that handle till it gets to a little arrow and then you open this so a stream of bubbles goes into the water. It doesn't get near as hot as now. But like I say, it's for heart cases or the feeble. Like Old Madam."

"What Old Madam?"

"Why, Old Madam that got herself drowned. She was takin' Naw Heem baths."

"Then Doctor Sandy had taken precautions with old Mrs. Chatham," Ellen said thoughtfully.

"Yessum, he sure did, and Miss Denise knew it, too." There was resentment in the woman's voice. "She's no call to blame Amy Lou either. She the same as said Amy Lou let Old Madam drown, and she got Amy Lou so upset she's quit her job here where she's worked ten solid years. Now I got to break in somebody new with all the other trouble." Still grumbling, she turned away and had reached the doorway when Ellen called her back.

"Is this the only stall where this"—she stopped and indicated the machine in the corner—"kind of bath can be given?"

"No'm, you can get you a fizzy bath in Number One. But that's all; just got two."

Ellen settled back with a grimace into the hot water, looking with unseeing eyes at the foot of her tub. Sandy had taken proper precautions. Then there was no reason to believe that she had had a sinking spell brought on by the heat! When the strap had broken she had been thrown off balance, and in trying to regain her position she must have struck the back of her head. So the strap was directly responsible for her death.

Had the water rotted the webbing? Tom didn't think so. If it had been no accident, as Charles had plainly thought, had someone cut the strap so the least strain would cause it to break? How could that have been done when the open archway that led into the bath stall was in full view of the women stretched out on the cooling boards waiting for massage? No one could have walked down the rubber matting path without running the gauntlet of feminine stares. Besides, the attendants popped in and out with the startling punctuality of a cuckoo clock.

Then the work must have been done after five o'clock when the baths closed for the day. Or maybe at night. Ellen sat up suddenly. *That* was why the horrible starched arm creature was on the stairs the night she was pushed! Then she shook her head. She was pushed after the fatal accident. What had the pusher been doing on the stairs? She gave it up.

She passed over the mice in the work basket and the stuck elevator as things that might happen any time. That brought her to Charles' stampeding wheel chair. That gave one furiously to think—but what? Ellen had followed Tom down into the rose garden as he examined the smashed chair with a flashlight. He had shrugged his shoulders over it. Denise was exploring the balcony floor as far as she could reach from a safe crouch inside the French doors when they had returned to Charles' room, but she shook her head, too.

There was nothing there.

Denise had pulled the damp towel robe around her beautiful legs and got to her feet. "I was having a bath, Tom," she explained quite unnecessarily, "when I heard Witless." She turned back toward the balcony. "I've felt over every inch I could reach from the door. I thought there might be a slickness or something." Her damp curls and the scrubbed look of her skin made Ellen think of a baby, sweet-smelling from a bath.

"See if you can find anything, Tom," she had urged, and followed Ranger to kneel again beside the open doors.

Ellen had looked at the slight elevation of the weather stripping. There was very little there to stop rolling wheels, and once over that, the balcony had a slight slope to the low rail for drainage. She had wondered at the vagaries of architects. It was a mercy that no one had fallen from there before; the thing was a decorative death trap.

At her elbow Isobel had said, "I planned to have Witless bring up the three potted oleanders today. Dora usually has them put on the balcony right at the first of the season, but she said she had forgotten them completely. They nearly fill the space and make it certain no one would go out. Of course, Charles wouldn't, but Janie or some other child might."

Ellen stopped to push up a bit in the tub and as usual, since the tub was close against the marble and there was no grip for the hands, she bumped her elbow soundly. She held the tingling crazy bone in her other

hand and muttered words between her teeth that relieved her feelings. Then she regarded the bumped
elbow thoughtfully. Surely she had been bumping the
right one daily in just that manner; why had the left
one caught it just now?

Still tenderly cradling the elbow, she looked more
attentively at the bath stall. Then she saw that Number Fifteen had the tub on the left side instead of the
right. She had made her usual slip, but the position of
the tub was reversed; it was on the left side here that
there was no grip for the hand. She noticed, too, that
the marble partition was a low one. Why was everything different here? Probably because of the window
in the end wall at the right.

Looking again at the marble, she leaned forward to
examine more closely the two spots about halfway up
the shining sheet of stone. About the size of a quarter,
they resembled the circles made by the occasional spit
balls fired during study hall. She thanked her stars that
the capacity of the biggest mouth limited the paper
wads she had to contend with to a much smaller size!
The spots were curious but she could think of nothing significant about them.

The fact that the tub was reversed in this stall made
for more privacy at least. One could often see
obliquely through the open arches to catch more than
a glimpse of the bathers therein. In Number Fifteen
the women cooling off could see only a stretch of
bare, tiled wall.

What she should be doing was relaxing in the
horribly hot water and getting her money's worth, she

told herself crossly. So she leaned back determined to do so, labelling the whole business of bathing in Number Fifteen as ridiculous and possibly a little morbid. She felt drowsy, leaning her head back into the grateful coolness of the wet towel. She contemplated her toes and thought of nothing.

She must have raised the toes in order to make the contemplation easier, for her balance shifted and that portion of her anatomy on which she reclined slipped suddenly on the smooth porcelain. The towel flopped over her face and she went under with a surge like a ship launching. Coming up, she clutched the sides of the tub and after a second or two clawed the towel out of her eyes and sat sputtering. Blast! She had whacked the same elbow again. She held the throbbing arm clutched tightly to her side. After a moment she released it and saw that there was blood on the fingers of her right hand.

She must have skinned herself that time. She investigated, but the elbow didn't feel skinned to her exploring fingers. She twisted around carefully, mindful of the ducking she had just experienced, to look at it. It wasn't skinned. Then where had the blood come from?

Looking again at her right hand, she found small cuts across all four fingers. On each side of the cuts, that still oozed a little blood, there were short abrasions like scratches. Her whole hand was slightly rusty. How in the world could the edge of the tub cut like that?

It couldn't have. Ellen sat up straight and began to

feel gingerly around the tub's curled back edge. Someone should have noticed such a thing before now. She
was momentarily as angry over such carelessness as
any of the voluble veranda complainers. There. Something, close under the rim. Her fingers exploring
could not tell her what it was, but it was more than a
roughness of cast iron.

Curious now, she climbed out of the hot water.
Dropping her wet turban to kneel on, she got down
on her knees to peer under the edge. A piece of metal
about four inches long and threaded nearly its full
length was stuck there under the rim of the tub with
a blob of black material she could not identify. But
the metal bit looked familiar. She felt that she had
often seen something like it, but what it was eluded
her.

She ran her fingers carefully over the threads and
found them sharp. When she looked at the investi-
gating finger it was slightly smeared with blood. She
had cut her fingers on the piece without a doubt. On
all fours now, she looked still closer at the puzzling
thing. In the center where a small bracket held the
threaded piece, something was caught. Pulling it out
carefully, she could make nothing of the tiny bit of
grayish fiber, but she poked it back in place as she had
found it.

Only then did she realize with a thrill of excitement
that she had discovered the means by which the safety
strap had been frayed. Whether Grandmother Chatham's death had been planned or was a fatal by-
product, the broken strap was no accident.

"For heaven's sake! Miss Ellen, what's the matter?"

" 'Fore the Lord, miss! Have you hurt yourself?"

Startled, she looked up to the archway. In the astonished eyes of Denise and Bella she saw herself as they must—wet, bare as the day she was born, insanely scrambling under the edge of the tub!

"I dropped something," she said lamely.

"And found it again, I hope?" Denise asked with exaggerated concern.

Bella judged that Ellen had gone far enough in her craziness. Picking up the rumpled tan sheet, she firmly folded Ellen into it and turned her toward the hot pack tables. But Ellen did not propose to be doused with hot water before she had looked into Bath Fourteen. She had not finished her investigation. She followed Bella meekly enough, with Denise treading on her heels, but as she passed the next arched doorway she contrived to stumble and send her dressing room key with its rattling plastic tag skipping inside.

As she stepped in to retrieve it, she glanced with elaborate casualness at the marble partition. Halfway down the stone there were two more quarter-sized spots dulling the gleaming polish. As she turned back to the rubber matting, she saw that Isobel, draped in her sheet, had joined the other two who watched her curiously.

CHAPTER X

The Chathams were concerned. They plainly thought that she was having delayed-action hysterics. And they could be right, Ellen agreed, unable to relax under the successive pourings and poundings. Her thoughts buzzed into and out of her brain like worker bees into the hive at the peak of the clover season. But laden with less pleasant harvests, she told herself.

Her mouth sagged open with astonishment when the drowsy, desultory conversation of Denise and Isobel on the cooling boards revealed that Charles was over in the men's baths getting his ten o'clock as if nothing had happened the night before.

"We thought he should stay in bed," Isobel said, pushing her towel back from her forehead, "but he said the bath would help his bruises and insisted on going."

"What he really said," Denise reported with relish, "was that he had come to this hellish place to bathe, and he stayed to bathe, and no circumstances either accidental or murderous were going to keep him from bathing!" Her violet eyes under the swathing towel glinted with laughter. "There was more along the same lines. Would you care to hear it?"

"That's quite enough," Isobel said. "Charles was really violent."

"If I'd had the narrow escape he did, I think I'd be violent, too," Ellen murmured.

Looking at Isobel and Denise lying side by side, she saw that they were as much alike as twins with their distinguishing hair concealed by the towel turbans and eyelids closed over sharp violet and dreaming black eyes. Their long white fingers, by coincidence laced together alike over the slow rhythm of their breathing, were identical. So too was their length, the two pairs of beautiful legs just reaching the end curlicues of the rattan couches. It was malfunctioning joints then, Ellen thought, that made Isobel, when erect, seem much shorter.

There *was* a difference; it was visible even with all expression relaxed and drained away. Ellen tried to capture the elusive impression by putting it into words. Polished—rough? Clear—vague? Sharp—dull? That was it. Denise was like a sharpened blade; Isobel a duller counterpart. Better still, Ellen thought, they were two identical sketches done in charcoal. Denise's lines had been defined and sharpened by the artist's fixative; Isobel's, untreated, had blurred and dissolved into vagueness.

Ellen realized that she was staring into Denise's face with a blind concentration. Her eyes focussed as the girl laughed.

"That was a really searching look," Denise said. "Did you find something else?"

Ellen colored in confusion. "I was only thinking," she said lamely.

The two Chathams stayed with her until she was stretched out on her own bed, having what they described as a nice little rest before dinner, the Eureka firmly following local custom with meals. The midday food was heavy and hearty, making a nap afterwards almost mandatory.

Ellen waited what she considered sufficient time after the door closed on them before springing out of bed. She wanted to talk to Tom at once. The reopening door caught her at the telephone.

"Miss Ellen, don't you want us to have your dinner sent up—" Denise stopped to stare at the empty bed. Her accusing gaze found Ellen with the receiver halfway to her ear, on her face the transparent innocence of a child with a fist in the cookie jar.

Ellen's invention let her down badly. "I thought I'd call for some water," she said lamely.

Denise glanced at the thermos pitcher on the table by the bed, which both of them knew was refilled morning and afternoon. Her voice was bland. "Sure you didn't drop something? Again?" The door shut just short of a slam.

It was twelve-thirty before Ellen found Tom. Central had grown tired of repeating, "Number, please?" during the ridiculous passage with Denise and was not disposed to hurry herself. The phone in his room did not answer, paging him in the lobby and on the veranda brought no results, and he was not drinking coffee—with real cream—at Dave's. Then she noticed the time, tried the dining room and found him.

He was audibly annoyed when he answered. "Why don't you come on down here and eat your dinner?" he demanded. "They just brought mine and I didn't get a single bite. Fried chicken, mashed potatoes with cream gravy and snap beans and okra. Mine's getting stone cold now," he added sourly.

Ellen repeated that what she had to tell was not for public dining rooms or even for telephones. And it couldn't wait.

"All right," Tom said reluctantly. "But you'd better make it good!"

Ellen met Tom at the elevators and led him to the sofa at the end of the hall. No one could possibly overhear them there, and besides, a schoolteacher's reputation being a delicate thing, perhaps she'd better lock the barn door. He listened without comment as she told of her discoveries in Fourteen and Fifteen, but he wore the fatuous smile of a doting parent when his child is turning in a bright performance. When she finished her story she stood up.

"Did I make it good enough?" she asked triumphantly.

Tom patted her back absently—and a trifle low, Ellen thought. "Plenty, plenty. Let's you and me go look again."

The desk clerk in the women's lobby reluctantly decided that it would be all right for him to go into the women's hall. There would be no more bathers there until one-thirty. Following Tom down the rubber matting, Ellen noticed the machine in the corner of

Number One and made a mental note to ask Sandy about the "fizzy baths," the "Naw Heems," as described and pronounced by Bella. Unconsciously noticing the numbers as she went she remembered wondering how the baths came out on pairs when there were fifteen of them. Ten, Eleven, Twelve, Fourteen —Fourteen? Where was Thirteen?

That was the way the stalls came out in pairs; there was no Number Thirteen. Then she stopped, looking unseeingly at the green rubber matting. She herself had been in Number Twelve on the day of old Mrs. Chatham's death. The noises she had heard had come, then, not from a nonexistent Thirteen but from Fourteen where she had found the marks on the marble. She stood trying to recall the sounds. A little pop, hardly audible? Her very keen ears had barely caught it. The murmur of running water? She remembered thinking that the bather was letting in a stream of cold and wishing that she had thought of cheating in a similar manner! No, it had been more like a murmur of conversation, but the bather must have been talking to herself, for Amy Lou had already gone up the row when Ellen heard it.

Tom stuck his head out of the last stall and called her impatiently. So she shook her head and gave it up.

"Listen, Sis." Tom's voice was concerned and serious as he stood leaning in the doorway of Fifteen waiting for her. "From now on you stay close to Papa, hear?"

Ellen looked at him, somewhat puzzled. The laughing twinkle was gone from his brown eyes; the quizzical eyebrows were drawn down into straight lines that emphasized every word like an underscore.

"Don't you ever—not even for just a minute—put that pretty neck of yours where somebody can wring it," Tom added.

"Why should anybody want to wring my neck, pretty or otherwise?" Ellen demanded. "And there ain't nobody here, Boss, but us detectives!"

Tom's mouth quirked in amusement, but his gaze was very serious.

"Probably not, but fifteen people could be hidden listening in this—this—" He searched for a word to describe the room-within-room complexity of the old building.

"Rabbit warren?" Ellen supplied helpfully.

"Okay, rabbit warren. Only I was going to say rats' nest. And stop putting words in my mouth!"

Ellen laughed.

"It's not a laughing matter," Tom insisted. "You know same as I do somebody tried murdering Charles last night, and you just got through telling me you'd found proof that old Miss Sara's accident wasn't one. You already got in that 'somebody's' hair once; be careful it ain't twice." He drew his booted foot up high against the wall and leaned in his favorite attitude. "There's no way to tell a murderer by looking at him, but if you could see inside his head it would be easy. Nothing but a seething mass of fears, working like maggots."

Ellen felt a little sick. "Tom, that's horrible—"

"Murder's never very nice, honey. But what I want

you to get is that once a man steps over that line that's labeled, 'Thou shalt not kill,' he's set apart forever from the rest of humankind. He's on a road without a turning that leads straight to death and destruction. And he's afraid every step of the way. Afraid he's not thought of everything; afraid he's left a tag that could unravel the whole plan; afraid of everybody and what everybody might know. So he gets busy trying to patch things up. Of course that's the way we get him. Ma always said if you didn't get the cake frosting smooth the first time, you might as well quit. Lord help the police if they ever have a murderer who lets bad enough alone!

"Now I don't know that you're a threat to that murderin' devil's safety, but he may think so, and killing doesn't come so hard a second time." Tom reached out and pulled Ellen close to him as he turned into the archway. His eyes had regained their usual twinkle as he finished his admonition. "So you stay close to Papa!"

There wasn't any doubt about it; she had found the method used to make the strap break. One had only to pull the under side of the webbing across the sharpened threads and the thing was done. It was stuck to the tub because a bather had no possible means of concealing the least thing about the person. But why leave it after the strap was weakened?

Tom found the answer to that. Pull as hard as he could with his fingers protected by a folded handkerchief, he could not loosen the bit of metal. He got down on his back and pulled, making a curious figure with his long legs halfway up the opposite wall. The sharpened metal had been left because ordinary strength couldn't budge it.

Sitting up and rubbing his reddened fingers, Tom thought aloud, "Stuff looks like tar or sealing wax, but it's sure got more stick than either one."

Ellen wondered why she should think of the Hamburger Hut. Then she remembered. Next door, she had been mildly interested in watching workmen on a remodeling job smear the backs of tiles with a black gluey substance. She had looked at the bucket, too, as she waited for the traffic light to change.

"Tom, what's 'mastic'?" she asked.

"Gluey dope they lay tiles and linoleum with," he answered absently. "Why?" Then his eyes narrowed. "No wonder he couldn't get it off again. He must not have known that stuff hardens faster than a miser's heart! Well, Bill's got to see this. I'll phone him soon's we go upstairs."

"Who's Bill and why has he got to see?" Ellen asked.

"Bill Anders, the sheriff. Remember I told you that was who I was talking to that first morning when you came downstairs? He's already started sniffing around. The sheriff mostly handles stuff of any size when the town's got no more police organization than this one has. Well, where are those spots you wanted me to see?"

Ellen went to stand at the side of the sheet of marble to catch the light on its surface. She moved closer to look more carefully, for the spots eluded her. She bent her head to look; she stood on tiptoe to look down. The spots were gone. Not even a finger smudge remained on the polished surface. Had a routine cleaning removed them or had that "someone" rubbed them off? She walked into Number Fourteen next door. There, too, the marble sheet gleamed spotless.

The clerk was gone from the desk when they went back to the women's lobby. She should have been there to schedule the one o'clock bathers, Ellen thought disapprovingly. Things were really going from bad to worse. The clerk's lunch tray, for instance, had been allowed to stand on the desk, looking as disgusting as picked bones and patches of cold vegetables can.

The sound that Ellen heard fitted right into the picture, too. Like someone being violently sick. She looked around in bewilderment; there was no one in the lobby or the hall. Again that horrible retching. Two long steps took Tom to the desk. He looked over and then swung himself to the floor behind. The desk clerk lay there prostrated, choking and vomiting.

Tom picked up the wretched woman and started outside with her, then, remembering the cooling couches close at hand, turned instead into the baths. Over his shoulder he directed Ellen, "Get Sandy down here."

She ran out into the center hall. In the doorway she nearly collided with two of the colored waiters supporting between them a man who barely kept his feet. His white sweating face and clutch at his throat spelled nausea. Ellen flattened herself against the wall to let them pass. What appalling thing had happened now?

One of the waiters spoke to her. "Go help 'em, ma'am. They sure need everybody."

When she got outside, she could believe help was needed. Violent nausea had struck the whole place. A man supporting himself by a hand on the grass beside the walk looked sick enough to die. Every chair on the veranda held a prostrate, retching patient. The doctors and nurses from the clinic were working rapidly, then handing people over to waiters from the dining room who were getting them upstairs into beds. Ellen caught sight of Sandy, bending over a woman lying in a glider, and made her way to him.

"Hey," she said, plucking childishly at his sleeve, "there's another one in the baths."

"Just one?" Sandy didn't even look around. With a sweep of his arm he summoned Willie and Witless, the elevator boys, and started them upstairs with the nearly unconscious woman. "Put her in the first bed you come to," he told them. Then he asked Ellen, "Is she bad, do you think? If she isn't, I'll get these two first. Look, you can take the kid upstairs to a room and then you stay up there and help. I'll send a nurse when I can."

Ellen propelled the green-faced Janie to the elevators. Through clenched teeth, the child muttered, "Hurry! Hurry!" On the second floor, she walked with a careful waddling motion, but the nausea caught her again. She leaned against the wall, her red hair ribbon bobbing over her sweating, convulsed face.

When the paroxysm was over, Ellen stripped her where she stood and got her to a bathroom. Then she put the child to bed, damp but clean.

As she tucked a sheet around Janie, Ellen heard another guest in an adjoining room begin weakly steering for the bath. When the wretch collapsed, groaning and retching, she ran to help. Then she held basins; she bathed sweating faces; she changed loathsome beds. After what seemed hours of this she began meeting a white-clad nurse and thankfully turned her patients over.

Sitting down on the sofa under the windows, she spoke firmly to her own churning stomach; there had been enough of that! As she supported her head on the back of her hand she saw that her watch showed six o'clock. What an afternoon! Hearing a step on the stairs, she looked up to see Susan wearily descending from the third floor. She dropped down on the sofa and likewise held her head.

"I've been making like a nurse for hours," Susan said in a tired voice. "Now I think I'll make like a patient."

"Don't you dare!" Ellen threatened fiercely.

"Twenty-seven people passed out in the dining room, or the halls, or the lobbies, or outside. All sick enough to die." Susan shuddered at her mental picture.

"Has anyone?" Ellen asked fearfully.

"Died? I don't think so, but I haven't seen Sandy since he yelled at me to come help when I was going past at one o'clock."

"What on earth happened?" Ellen roused herself to ask. "What caused it? I haven't heard a thing except, 'Hey! C'mere quick!' or 'Hey! Rush the basin!'"

"It must be food poisoning. Nearly everybody who ate in the dining room got sick as a horse." Susan elaborated morbidly, "Sick as a great, big horse."

CHAPTER XI

Looking in on her erstwhile patients the next morning, Ellen found everyone much better. Janie was almost as good as new, sitting up in bed and poking spoonsful of scrambled eggs into her mouth while her eyes followed the adventures of Captain Marvellous.

"Hi, Miss Ellen," she said, her eyes returning to the colored panels. "Say, let's us and Tom be detectives like Captain Marvellous and find out what's happening in this stinkin' old hotel!"

"Janie!" Mrs. Jeris' voice preceded her tottering steps from the adjoining bath.

"Maybe not now," Janie conceded. "But it sure was yesterday, 'specially where people had—"

"Janie! That will be all!" Mrs. Jeris pulled her black and white housecoat around her and sank into a chair. Ellen thought her face, with the skin pulled tighter over the cheek bones and the prominent nose, with her bird bright eyes deep in their sockets, looked more like a magpie's than ever.

"Thank you for what you did for Janie yesterday, Miss Knowles," the woman said. "I was completely prostrated. You know how bad off I was never to have had a thought for my poor baby! Doctor said I was undoubtedly the sickest patient he treated. Just a shade more—" Mrs. Jeris shrugged her shoulders with gloomy relish.

Before Ellen could say anything, Mrs. Jeris asked, "And how did you escape, dear Miss Knowles? Did you have a premonition? Or"—with an arch tone in her voice—"did you go some place with that fascinating Mr. Ranger?"

To her confusion Ellen could feel that hateful blush she had recently acquired mounting into her face. "We—that is, I was just late getting down," she said. "Is everyone better this morning?"

"As far as I've heard. Oh, no, the nurse said Mr. Charles Chatham was pretty sick still."

Janie's spoon scraped around the plate and, arriving at her mouth empty, drew her eyes from the comic book. "I'm ready to get up, Mom," she announced. "Then we'll go find Tom, Miss Ellen."

"You're going to stay right in that bed, young lady, till the doctor sees you and says it's all right." Her voice was positive, but Ellen said a hasty good-bye, forseeing the usual mother daughter debate with Janie the winner.

As she passed the next open door, her eye was caught by a glimpse of Hampton Potts, languid in lavender pajamas, reclining against piled-up pillows.

"Dear Miss Ellen!" he called in his fluting voice. "Be an angel of mercy and come talk to me."

"I was an angel of mercy yesterday," Ellen went

in to lean on a chair back after refusing to sit down, "and I don't care for it."

"Utterly horrible." Hampton shuddered visibly. "Doctor Doulton said I was undoubtedly the sickest patient he treated. Just a breath more!" Hampton raised his eyes with the air of having received a last minute reprieve. "I told Dora just now that I wished for her stamina. She's carrying on like the brave little soldier she is, with the whole place buzzing around her ears like hornets this morning."

"Did she know what had happened?" Ellen asked.

"No. No one seems to know." Hampton shook his head. "It couldn't have been the food—"

"Why not? That seems most likely."

"No, some of the guests who ate dinner with us at the same time didn't get sick," Hampton argued. "Dora didn't and she sat at my very table. Mrs. Horton, too—you know, that large gray-haired woman on the third floor?—she wasn't sick either. She went up a bit early to take a nap and slept through everything! Imagine!"

As soon as she could, Ellen escaped. The woman next to Janie was better; so were Isobel and Denise back in their own rooms on the third floor now that the worst was over. In fact, Denise looked as blooming as ever, Ellen thought with some envy of the resilience of youth. But Charles Chatham was still alarmingly ill, to the concern of his sister and his niece.

As soon as she could, Ellen headed for the dining room. The big room was deserted except for Sandy, who sat at a corner table, supporting his tousled head with one hand while he aimlessly stirred his coffee. He glanced up as she came in and beckoned her over.

"Once I read a fairy tale about a man who knew not fear," he said. "Are you a direct descendant?"

As a good English teacher should, Ellen spotted the illusion. "You mean the one about the man who couldn't shudder," she corrected promptly. "Only he could. They put a lot of little wet fishes in his bed, and who wouldn't?" Sandy looked slightly puzzled as she went on. "But I'm not like him. I'm simply scared to death."

"But you aren't scared to eat?" Sandy indicated the empty room with a sweep of his hand. "Lord knows I don't blame them. No one in his right senses—and that includes you—would eat here after yesterday."

"Coffee and dry toast," Ellen told the hovering waiter. That order should be hard to tamper with.

"Coffee is a favorite medium for poisoners," Sandy remarked dryly.

Ellen was indignant. "Sandy Doulton, this is no time or place for feeble humor!"

"Of course it isn't, and I apologize. Maybe I have a touch of male hysterics." Sandy turned his coffee cup around and around absently. "How did you manage to escape yesterday?"

Ellen told him of the discoveries she had made and of the half-hour she and Tom had spent in the baths. It didn't seem to surprise Sandy so much as confirm what he had already suspected.

"I never thought of looking under the rim of the tub," he said.

"There wouldn't have been anything to see there if the mastic hadn't stuck tighter than the person who used it anticipated!" Then Ellen remembered. "Janie's skates!" she said loudly.

Sandy started and spilled the coffee he was dribbling from his spoon into the cup. "Janie's skates?"

"That's what that piece is," Ellen nodded positively. "I kept thinking I'd seen something like that piece of metal stuck under the tub. It's that part of a roller skate that makes the foot clamps adjust. Janie said a piece was gone from her new skates. So it had to be someone here at the hotel!"

Sandy looked at her strangely. "Did you ever have any idea that all this wasn't inside stuff?"

They sat in silence as the waiter brought Ellen's order. Then she remembered the special baths she had wanted to ask him about.

"That's right; Nauheim type," Sandy told her. "We use a controlled stream of carbon dioxide and a much lower temperature. It's useful in certain kinds of circulatory disease, in heart cases, and with the aged or feeble."

"Like old Miss Sara?"

"Yes, she was having them."

"Then why did Denise accuse you of carelessness? Of failing to consider her age and condition?"

"It's natural to lash out at the nearest person when you get hurt, whether they had anything to do with the hurt or not," Sandy said, his eyes on the coffee he poured from the end of the spoon. "You know, a lot of Good Samaritans get smacked for their good intentions." He added, "Anyway, she's sore at me for some reason. Just this summer. We used to be good friends and sometimes I figured maybe she and I—" His voice and the thought trailed off into silence together.

That half-confidence explained a good many things to Ellen. She eyed the coffee before her dubiously. Then she took a cautious sip with every taste bud on the alert for an alien flavor. Over the rim of the cup her eyes met Sandy's, and she grinned weakly as she put the coffee down again.

"It's all right, really," he assured her. "I personally threw every bit of food in the kitchen into the incinerator early this morning after I finished testing. Dora Martingale got in a whole new set of stuff, and nobody could've tampered with it, for the sheriff's got a man in there now." He added grimly, "And when we catch Amy Lou's Dorrie—"

Ellen had so many questions to ask she couldn't get them sorted. "Sandy, what was it—food poisoning? Ptomaine?"

"Oh no, our joker didn't want anyone killed this time, it seems. Croton oil in the mashed potato and gravy; an emetic in the coffee."

"What about Amy Lou's Dorrie?"

"She's one of the maids and works sometimes in the kitchen, too. She's Amy Lou's daughter—you know the woman who worked in the baths until Denise upset her so about old Miss Sara's drowning that she left— She didn't show up this morning and nobody can remember that they saw her yesterday afternoon. She didn't go home last night, so it's plain she's involved somehow. Tom's looking for her, and we'll get it out of her what happened. Someone's going to sweat for this, but plenty."

Sandy sighed and pushed his chair back. "Well, there's still the whole second floor to look at." He straightened his shoulders with a tired shrug. "I'm worried about Mr. Charles. That was a hell of a thing to happen to a man with peptic ulcers." Pausing by her chair, he added, "Let's tell anyone who asks that it must have been ptomaine." He nodded at her agreement and went on out.

Ellen sat for a long time in the deserted room with only her empty cup for company. She was tired and she felt completely stupid. She wandered out into the lobby deserted by all but the desk clerk gloomily reading the bulletin he had just pinned up. It announced, "No guests of this hotel will be permitted to leave until further notice. Signed: William Anders, Sheriff."

Next morning lean individuals wearing deputy badges lounged on every floor with one eye on the stairs and the other on the elevators. The recovered guests demanded loudly and collectively that they be permitted to depart. They threatened the harried clerk with their lawyers and their congressmen until he wrung his hands and his confidential voice sank to a placating whisper. Luggage piled up near the doors and the buzz of shrill angry conversation went on interminably.

Ellen sighed and made for the dining room. Quiet

was a commodity that the Eureka was fresh out of, apparently. But the big empty dining room was not only quiet; it was dreary and dismal in the grey light of the rainy morning. She hesitated in the doorway, but the smell of hot coffee decided her. The head waiter ushered her to a window table where she looked out on flowers flattened and mud-spattered as she ate ham and grits with rusty gravy.

When a pleased voice asked, "How are you, sugar?" she pretended that she did not know the question was for her and did not turn around. Conceited creature, she told herself, so sure she would be tickled to death to see him again!

And aren't you? Startled at the implications of her mental question, Ellen blushed rosily and becomingly to her ears as she looked up at Tom, resplendent in dark blue gabardines and black boots with white inlays.

He beamed and said softly, "Why, Ellen! Why, honey!" as if she had explained everything. He dropped into the chair beside her, thrusting his long legs to fold under the table.

Ellen was obscurely furious at both herself and Tom. She directed a tirade at him that surprised them both. She blamed him for half the things that had happened; for the way he didn't tell her anything; for the failure to stop the mad antics at the hotel. She was nasty and sarcastic.

Tom protested, "Aw, Ellen, don't be like that," as she paused for breath. She turned toward him quickly, having something particularly scorching to add, and elbowed her coffee squarely into his embroidered shirt pockets.

Aghast, she flew at the brown tide with her napkin. Tom said nothing; she found nothing to say. Dabbing at the stains on the beautiful shirt, she ventured a quick glance up into his face. It was very serious, but around his eyes the crinkles of laughter grew deeper and deeper. Her own lips curled in spite of herself.

"You certainly work up to a wicked climax!" Tom said when their laughter had subsided. "Besides, you made me forget one way and another what I was going to tell you."

Ellen looked up from making circles on the wet tablecloth with her water glass. Tom's voice was grim now.

"Charles Chatham has just died. The sheriff is going to ask for a John Doe warrant for manslaughter."

Ellen's eyes filled with tears and she felt a pang of pity for the man who had endured years of pain only to reach surcease in death. The tears were for the girls, who would have another sorrow added to their recent grief.

"I was thinking about Isobel and Denise," she said, wiping her eyes childishly on the back of her hand. "Charles' death was due then to this food—" She didn't think Sandy's warning applied to Tom.

"Yes; directly due to this blamed monkey business. But I should have said warrants. Bill's going to get another on account of what you found in the baths yesterday. For old Miss Sara; same charge."

Ellen said nothing; in fact she didn't seem to have heard. She was looking at the water glass with fascinated eyes. As she lifted it the concave base plucked at the damp cloth beneath it, held by the slight vacuum inside. She looked from the tumbler to the round spot it had made on the cloth.

"Something on a vacuum cup," she told him raptly. "That could have made the spots! Like the gadget to hold fishing poles on top of cars that I saw in the hardware store window yesterday!"

CHAPTER XII

Tom listened to her explanation patiently but with an air of bewilderment. "But what's the point of all that?" he asked.

"You don't agree that the spots on the marble could have been made that way?" she asked in her turn.

"Could have, but what's the sense of it? Who did it?"

It was her turn to say nothing.

Tom went on, "It seems more reasonable to me that we have some guy planning accidents and getting more than he bargained for."

"You said yourself that murder was seldom reasonable!"

"No, and it isn't, but two times out of twice, the guy that has the most to gain by monkey business is the guy who starts monkey business."

"Then you think it was—?"

"Sure. The sheriff's asked him to step around to his office this afternoon. Maybe we'll find Amy Lou's Dorrie by then and she'll have something to add."

Ellen thought her inspired reconstruction had received cool treatment, but as she considered it, she agreed with Tom. It did seem unnecessarily fancy, and it certainly began nowhere and ended the same place. She shrugged mentally and changed the subject.

"Tom, have you seen the Chatham girls? Since, I mean? Do you think I should go? After all, I'm only an acquaintance—"

"Why don't you go this afternoon? Sandy and Doc are up there now, and they have to make arrangements. It's kind of hard on two women alone," he said with sympathetic understatement. Then he patted her shoulder briskly and went away again, presumably to look some place for Amy Lou's Dorrie.

Late in the afternoon when her bath was over, Ellen changed to a thin dark dress and went up to the third floor to pay her last respects to Mr. Charles. She wondered what she could say to Isobel and Denise; there wasn't much to offer the sorrowing beside the usual kindly meant banalities. She pieced together bits offered by the chattering coteries of the veranda to add to her own impression of the dead man. She imagined him when the leonine head had been black rather than silver, when brisk, lean young strength had moved the immobile legs. The women whispered that his physical beauty and attraction had been irresistible. His flexible voice, with more stops than an organ, had resounded from courthouse to capitol and his political future glittered with promise.

Then "something happened." That was to quote the whispers. A mysterious accident kept Charles more dead than alive in hospitals for months. During that time old Miss Sara moved her entire family, Isobel, the younger son, Doctor Denis Chatham, and his young wife to the Georgia plantation. There Denise was born and there the young mother died. Tragedy stalked the family again, for Doctor Denis accidentally shot himself while hunting. To the diminished household Charles returned eventually, white of hair and chained to his wheel chair, his wrecked body symbolic of his wrecked life, Ellen thought.

Susan, looking subdued, answered her tap at the door and led her across the room to Denise, who sat beside the window filled with Isobel's flowers. She was red-eyed and stricken, smoothing a damp handkerchief in her hands. Isobel was nowhere in sight.

"Doctor Doulton put her to bed," Susan whispered in answer to the unspoken question. She was perfectly ghastly and she couldn't stop shaking.

Denise looked up blankly when Ellen spoke to her, but in the middle of the first sentence her eyes filled with tears and she dropped her head into her hands, sobbing.

"She's held up so well all day," Susan said over the bowed head to Ellen. "She's been wonderful." She held the shaking shoulders. When the sobs had subsided, they washed the tear stained face and encouraged Denise to talk to relieve the tension that held her.

"It's been so overwhelming a shock, Denise." Ellen shook her head in sympathy. "Even when you're expecting the death of a—"

"But we weren't expecting it," Denise interrupted. "Sandy wasn't even, no matter what he says now!

He made another mistake, and Isobel and I will have to bury it like the first. His license to practice should be taken away! I told him Uncle Charles was awfully sick, but he's like all doctors; he doesn't think anyone but an M.D. can tell the difference between dog bite and diptheria!" Denise said wildly.

Then her mood veered like a sailboat in a gust of wind and she wept again. "But I shouldn't blame any-one more than I blame myself. I didn't really think he was going to die. I didn't go in to see him even—"

"Sandy didn't neglect Mr. Charles; I'm sure of that." Ellen spoke soothingly. "But you must remem-ber that he had dozens of patients in an emergency that would have taxed the resources of a large hospital. Did Mr. Charles seem terribly sick right after dinner that day?" Ellen asked the question hoping to divert Denise's thoughts. Surely she shouldn't go on in that mixed state of rage and grief.

"I don't know. I was too sick myself," Denise said. "I got to my room before— But I didn't know Uncle Charles was bad off until later. Sandy said he was weak, but he didn't think it was critical—he said he would watch on account of Uncle Charles' bad stom-ach."

"He—Sandy, I mean—sent a nurse as soon as he could," Susan said. "I heard him tell Miss Liz to go stay with him."

"That batty old bag! Another one of Sandy's mis-takes!" Denise's violet eyes flashed with scorn.

"She's queer at times, but you know she's a fine nurse and still perfectly capable of watching a patient.

You know, too, Denise, that she took every care of
Mr. Charles, so you can just stop storming about
that!" Susan said sharply.

Denise looked at Susan in a mild surprise. "I suppose she did what could be done," she said reluctantly.
"I don't suppose Sandy trusted her with the medicines,
and she did help Uncle Charles through the night and
all that next day. Isobel said so, anyway."

"Did he suffer very much?" Ellen asked Susan
softly, but Denise heard and answered.

"Oh, a great deal. Sandy gave him stuff, but he had
violent stomach pains and cramps and that awful
vomiting we all had—" Denise wept again. When the
tears stopped, she said in a flat and colorless voice,
"First Grandmother and then Uncle Charles."

"You and Isobel have each other," Ellen soothed.

Denise looked at her quickly, her eyes like violets
after a rain. There was a puzzled expression in their
depths. Her gaze dropped to her twisting fingers and
her voice hurried. "It would be better if I were alone.
I wouldn't be so frightened."

Ellen and Susan looked at each other in consternation.

"I can't *stand* it any longer! I haven't told anyone,
but I'm afraid, afraid! Grandmother had noticed it.
She threatened Grandmother; I heard her! She wanted
to go to a specialist in the East, a doctor who has had
success with cases like hers, but Grandmother thought
it was useless. It would just get her hopes up to dis-
appoint her again. Isobel told her she'd get the money
in spite of her. She said Grandmother would be sorry.

She raved!"

There was terror in the swift sentences and a great urgency. "I know Uncle Charles knew something; he talked like he expected to die— Last night I woke up and she was standing by my bed! She just stood there. I was so frightened I couldn't move."

"You're all wrought up, Denise." Ellen made her voice sound more matter of fact than she felt." All this has been dreadful for you both; no one could be quite normal in such a situation. Isobel is shocked and grieved, so of course she couldn't sleep. She didn't want to waken you, that's all." She added firmly, "You must stop talking like this. Isobel loves you as if you were her own daughter."

"But I was afraid! I'm still afraid!" Denise's voice grew shriller. "I got up and locked the door after she went away and this morning she asked me why. And she looked so strange." She pulled at the damp handkerchief distractedly. When she looked up at Ellen again, the violet eyes were wide and strained. "If I didn't have to be here alone—would you stay with me?"

"Of course I will, child. Susan, you get her ready for bed while I run down the hall a moment. I promise, one of us will stay with you until you feel better." Ellen's most practical voice tried to sweep away the atmosphere of hysteria she felt in the room.

"I'm afraid, I'm afraid," Denise repeated in a whimper that ended in a childish sniff. After a moment she shook back her hair, wiped her eyes and followed Susan into the bedroom. There was something pa-

thetic and young in the way she determinedly straightened her shoulders and lifted her chin.

Ellen located a nurse on the third floor and told her
Denise needed help. Then she followed her rattling
uniform back to the Chatham suite. There the nurse
went to the medicine cabinet in the bathroom and,
taking a small bottle from a shelf, tipped out two tablets and dissolved them in a glass of water. Then she
handed the glass to Ellen and replaced the bottle.

"It's a mild sedative that Doctor Doulton prescribed
for old Miss Sara," she explained. "Doctor gave two
of the tablets to Miss Isobel an hour ago to get her to
rest for a while. There's no need calling them up here
again when I know they would give Miss Denise the
same thing."

Ellen looked at the nurse doubtfully.

"I'll call, if you insist." The nurse's voice mirrored
her impatience, but she went to the telephone. She
held a short conversation, then nodded. "Doctor says
it's okay." And she went on out.

Denise looked sharply at the glass, but when Ellen
told her what it was, she drank it docilely enough and
lay back on her bed. Ellen returned the glass to the
bathroom. Then she went out into the little sitting
room to answer the door, leaving Susan with Denise.

Answering the door proved to be the task she had
thought it would be. A great many friends and acquaintances came in genuine kindness of heart and
even more than the usual number came in varying
stages of poorly disguised curiosity. After a time Ellen
noticed that Susan had come from the bedroom and

was arranging the flowers that had been arriving. When she raised a questioning eyebrow, Susan came over to murmur, "She said she was getting sleepy, and she was sorry she had been such a fool. And for me to get on out and let her take the damned nap!"

That sounded more like the usual Denise, Ellen thought as she went to the door again. A glance down at her watch showed her that she was going to miss another meal. Her days were misery, mishap and malnutrition! Dora Martingale's arrival at that moment was almost more than she could bear.

Miss Martingale grieved for Isobel and Denise. She herself had been so fond of Charles, too. Such a distinguished man at one time. Then she took the opportunity to tell Ellen how completely wonderful they all thought she was. Dora, herself, couldn't thank her enough for the help she had given during the awful day before. Ellen's attitude toward the hotel and the baths and the Doultons in the face of this total disaster—! Well, Dora, from the bottom of her heart, considered it self-sacrificial and truly Christian!

It was deep twilight when Susan's grandmother came, and, murmuring excuses to her, Ellen scurried to her room for her purse, planning to find a cup of coffee at least. At the elevators the long deputy leaning with one foot on the wall behind him watched her without interest, then turned to look out of the windows. Across the hall from her room the linen closet door stood half open and the starched uniform of a maid bent over the laundry chute as she forced a billowing bundle of soiled linen down it.

Ellen stood inside her room with her hand still on
the door knob. She wondered why the maid's occupa-
tion had struck her as peculiar. What was strange
about a maid with an armful of dirty sheets? But surely
under the eyes of Martingale, the martinet, beds were
changed earlier in the day than this! No one had been
allowed to leave, so there could be no rooms to make
up after departing guests. Perhaps the maids were late
because of the press of work from the days before.

Still, it was odd. She stood at the side of the door
and looked through the open louvers. Now the maid
was taking an armload of sheets from the shelves and
going down the short cross hall. Almost at once she
reappeared again with another great armful of linen to
poke down the chute. Getting more linen from the
closet, she again went down the hall out of sight.
Apparently this was a wholesale changing of beds.

Down by the elevators, the deputy found domestic
details boring and went back to his window gazing.
It seemed to Ellen that the maid with her arms filled
with more laundry didn't walk back quite so briskly.
Did she look around the bundle that hid her face to
see if the deputy still watched? And what was there
about that momentary glimpse at once furtive and
familiar?

It took longer to punch the bundle down the chute
this time, too. The maid at last straightened up and
went into the linen closet. Ellen could just see in the
gathering darkness of the hall that she was taking
folded linens from a lower shelf to stack them on a
higher. Then she took them from the shelf on which

she had just placed them and shifted them again to a lower! She dropped one pile as she leaned over and did not bother to pick them up again. She was watching the deputy through the crack of the open door! Directly opposite, Ellen stood close to her louvers and watched the watcher.

Apparently satisfied that the eagle eye of the law was something less than alert, the maid slipped out of the closet and flattened herself against the wall. Then, protected by the half open door, she crept silently down the stairs to the baths!

Ellen pulled hard at her own door, but even as her mouth opened to call out to the deputy, she shut both mouth and door and hurriedly considered the situation. The maid would be whole flights and floors away on her furtive errand while Ellen tried to explain to the man. And what could that perambulating case of hookworm do that she herself couldn't do as well or better? After all, it was only another woman to follow.

She snatched a small flashlight from the bedside table and kicked off her pumps. The deputy still looked down into the darkening street, so she opened her door carefully and boldly stepped across the hall to the protecting linen closet door. Just as she reached it, the young man down the hall stretched lazily and started a patrol. Ellen began to get her story ready, for she could not close the door without being seen, and he would not fail to see her lurking and in stocking feet as he passed. She drew a deep breath of relief when he turned back at the cross hall, paying no more than a casual glance to the open door. Apparently he thought the maid was still working behind it.

When his back was safely turned, Ellen flew down the hall into the shadows on the stairs. She was just out of sight when the man turned to look down the now empty hall and pressed the light switches. On the landing all her resolution could not force her down that darkling flight where she had encountered the starched sleeves. Maybe those sleeves had been part of a maid's uniform!

Then from below, her excellent ears heard the faintest click. Unless there were two persons roaming in the near-darkness, she was alone on the stairs. The mysterious maid had reached the Lobby and was moving about there. Ellen's fears replaced by curiosity again, she slipped silently down the next flight to the landing that overlooked the Lobby.

She could see nothing, and her reborn courage was not great enough to take her down to the lobby floor where the chairs and desks and potted plants would furnish cover for an army of ambushed assassins. She stood helplessly peopling the dark with terrors as she saw and heard nothing. Defeated, she strained into the gloom once more and nearly cried out as she saw a pinpoint of light appear, disappear, then shine faintly. She had heard the lock of the tunnel door! Someone moved inside the tunnel!

CHAPTER XIII

Ellen stood in the blackness outside the tunnel door for a long time. Her common sense, for which she was normally notable, told her how foolhardy she was; reminded her that the usual reward for such foolhardiness was a sharp blow on the back of the head; demanded to know what she hoped to discover in the tunnel anyway.

"Probably how it feels to get my head bashed in," she told herself grimly." But go ahead; rush in, Fool!" And with that she turned the knob, holding back the latch so there would be no betraying click and inched around the door, her whole body tense to meet descending violence. Nothing happened. When she could breathe again, she saw a tiny light flicking cautiously far ahead.

The floor sloped under her feet with sickening suddenness. A wheel chair ramp, of course. She moved slowly; the tunnel could not be very long. The Eureka and its baths were on one corner; the Thermal and its baths on the next. The hotel was on the opposite side of the street, the baths on the same side as the Eureka's. That had been the reason for a tunnel from the Ther-

mal to its baths, she remembered, so guests wouldn't
have to go out on the street to reach the hot and
healing waters. She crept along from brick to brick
in the damp wall, keeping her eyes on the pencil of
light ahead.

Then her ears picked up the sharp sibilance of whis-
pering voices. The maid was meeting someone! An
inch at a time she stole closer, but the distance was too
great to do more than distinguish two voices, one
deeper which seemed to be doing most of the murmured talking. Had she scared herself half to death to
eavesdrop on a waiter's wooing!

She had kept close to the right hand wall, her
fingers following the cool oblongs of the bricks as she
passed. When her hands found a sharp angle, she realized after a confused moment that she had reached the
cross tunnel running under the street from the Thermal to its baths. By crossing the intersecting tunnel at
an angle until she struck the opposite wall and then
following that wall back, she could get closer to the
whisperers and still remain concealed by the tunnel
mouth. She decided at once to try it.

She started across before her courage failed her. She
shivered in the palpable darkness, feeling that any instant she would encounter disaster, but after a few
bad moments of feeling lost in nothingness, she felt the
bricks of the opposite wall under her fingers. The
voices grew louder as she crept along the tunnel, near-
ing the corner.

The flashlight threw a wavering monstrous shadow
on the dim walls, magnified out of all proportion until

it bore no human resemblance. With any movement of the source of light it mocked and moved like an evil idiot. A sudden movement of the unseen hand sent the menacing shade leaping up the wall faster than the genie escaping his bottle. Ellen cowered in terror, her arm covering her face. Then her sense of hearing strained forward, trying to pick words from the susurrus of sibiliant sound.

There was a familiarity about the maid's voice; her talk rose and fell in a cadence that just eluded memory. If she could get closer in some way! Ellen's fingers explored the wall. At arm's length she found a shallow depression, apparently backed by a counter or shelf at about her shoulder height. It was probably the bath clerk's niche, Ellen thought, and it must extend some way toward the tunnel mouth. If she could flatten herself into that—

But the niche was already occupied. Ellen's feet stumbled over something at the instant her groping hands encountered it. Under one hand was that horrible, familiar feel of starched cloth; the other sent a puzzling message to her brain, growing numb with terror. Her fingers felt hair . . . hair in tight, small braids. . . .

With a fluttering sigh, Ellen fainted for the first time in her life. She had found Amy Lou's Dorrie. And Amy Lou's Dorrie was colder than the wall she leaned against.

The black waves of horror that had submerged her ebbed slowly away, but she continued to lie on the tunnel floor with her eyes closed tight against the grisly darkness that rocked and roared around her. Then hearing, last of the senses to leave and first to return, picked up again the waves of murmured talk, louder now with the overtones of anger and protest. Incredulously Ellen realized that her collapse must have been noiseless, that she was not discovered. The tunnel floor was cold and hard under her cheek, but she was afraid to shift her position. What if she brought the horror in the niche tumbling stiffly down?

She could hear the voices plainly. "You bungling fool!" said the man's voice furiously, "you've gone too far with everything! I plan accidents— you produce manslaughter!"

"But that's what I've been telling you! I haven't done a thing more than we planned!"

"Planned, hell! All I wanted to do was needle the Doultons and make their plant look as dilapidated and inefficient as it is. But you drown an old lady and poison her son!"

"And I tell you I never went near Aunt Sara! All I did in the baths was fix the thermostats once— and on the men's side. I didn't touch that safety strap. And I put exactly as much oil as you said. Don't you try to saddle me with all the blame!"

Ellen wasn't really surprised that the woman's voice was that of Dora Martingale. Lying on the cold bricks, she even felt a kind of satisfaction. She had thought her an odious fraud from the first.

"It was your idea in the first place."

"And you jumped at it!" the hostess answered. Her

voice changed, grew sirupy and plaintive. "I did it for you, Horace. To help you get started. How can you blame me so?"

The man's voice was derisive. "You mean you saw a chance to get back at Doulton for not wanting to marry you, you frustrated spinster!"

Ellen had heard enough. Crabbing cautiously backwards. She crawled away from the niche and struck across the tunnel to the opposite side again. Strangely enough, she was no longer afraid. She felt only contempt for the two, still blaming each other and still unaware, she was sure, that they had been overheard.

She felt her way back down the tunnel to the women's lobby, not even caring greatly if the bickerers heard her. She was on the stairs again before she asked herself how the two were responsible for Amy Lou's Dorrie. But she was too weary, too sickened to think about it. All she wanted was to find Tom and tell him how right he had been.

Too tired for subterfuge, she plodded up the stairs and down the hall. The deputy, hearing her, turned around, and she was fleetingly amused at the surprise and indecision on his face. Before he could think what to do about her, she slipped into her room and locked the door. She sat down the edge of her bed, blankly staring at a flower in the carpet. She would try to find Tom when her knees stopped trembling.

When a knock rattled her door, she straightened up, demanding to know who was there. She was sure it was the deputy belatedly inquiring her business in the baths, but Tom's ungrammatical, "It's me," sent her flying to let him in.

"Where in thunder have you been?" he demanded."
I swear you can disappear faster'n pie at a church
supper."

Ellen burst into sudden floods of tears. The next
few moments grew confused. She saw Tom's scowl
break into consternation, and then they were both in
the big old platform rocker, her face hidden in his
shirt front while he patted and soothed her with,"
"There, there now, sugar," much as he would gentle a
pony. Meanwhile he rocked resoundingly back and
forth over a squeaking floor board.

At last Ellen sat up and dried her eyes. She turned to
get to her feet, but Tom's arm tightened around her to
keep her where she was.

"Feel better?" he asked comfortably. "My Ma always said a good cry was worth twenty dollars to a
woman."

"Oh, Tom, you fool," she told him helplessly. "I'm
not crying for fun or twenty dollars. I'm tired and
scared half to death and there was Amy Lou's Dorrie—" She stopped with a long shudder.

Tom sat up with a jerk, his eyes intent and his
mouth falling into straight lines. "Begin," he said
tersely. "I shoulda known you'd been up to something."

Ellen told. "And you were right, Tom. It was
Fowler all the time."

"I was right about something else, too, but you
didn't remember that." He looked down at her and
shook his head. "About not going anyplace alone,

remember? I said you might meet a murderer?" He dumped her from his lap without ceremony and stood up. "Get your stuff and come on."

"Where are we going?" Ellen asked meekly.

"I'm going to get the sheriff out of bed. You're going to spend the night with the Chathams and Susan. And if you so much as stick your nose out of the door—" The sternness of tone was somewhat relieved by a brisk spank." We couldn't get a thing out of Fowler this afternoon, but this'll bust him wide open. Only I will say, sugar, you got more spunk than sense!"

In the Chathams' sitting room, Susan was curled up like a kitten in a big chair. "Where've you been, Ellen?" she asked, blinking sleepily. "I thought you'd never get back."

"That same thought occurred to me once or twice," Ellen murmured, "But never mind now; I'll tell you all about it in the morning. How are Isobel and Denise?"

"Both still asleep, but you look, too." Susan yawned widely.

Isobel was turning restlessly, but her regular breathing showed that she slept. Denise lay motionless, completely relaxed, one hand tucked under her cheek. Ellen got a blanket and, eyeing the small chair by the bedside, decided she would be just as much protection on the settee and far more comfortable. The whole thing was just a gesture anyway. Then she kicked off her slippers, stretched out and began repeating some of the longer ballads, her time-honored method of getting to sleep.

Ellen turned over on the settee, opening her tightly shut eyes. Sleep would never come while her mind churned like five quarts of cream on butter-making day. The moonlight showed her Susan sleeping in the big chair, her bare feet hanging over the arm. Ellen's eyes roamed over the dim room, picking out the shadowy masses of chairs and desk, following the lighter bands of woodwork to the oblong of the white door. That oblong was oddly foreshortened— its top line at an angle with the wall— The door was slowly opening!

She lay rigid, her eyes on the creeping intruder while terror turned the blood in her veins to lead, weighing her to the couch in a paralysis of fear. Her tongue clove to the roof of her dry mouth and the beating of her heart mounted thunderingly in her ears. The tall white figure was in the room now. Susan— but the high back and wings of her chair hid that defenseless sleeper from the peering gaze that the turning head indicated. There was nothing to shield Ellen.

From the moving form she heard a tiny crackle of sound as it approached the settee. Ellen tried to scream, but no frantic urgings from her brain could unlock her throat. She thought despairingly, "I've always known I wasn't the screaming kind!" With an impulse to hide from the advancing nightmare, she closed her eyes, but the lids would not stay down. Through her lashes she watched the figure come closer. Then her straining ears identified that swish of sound; it was the crackle of starched cloth.

With no care to be noiseless, the intruder swung a chair around to the side of the settee, sat down and bent over. One large hand was laid on Ellen's sweating forehead and the other picked up her wrist! She might have voiced the rising scream then, but sheer bewilderment kept her as dumb as the terror it had replaced. There was kindness in the stroking hand and competence in the firm press of the fingers. Then as the forefinger found the racing blood in her wrist, she understood. The intruder was checking her pulse!

Ellen's eyes opened wide as her arm was laid across her chest and the blanket was tucked about her body expertly. The movement brought an elaborately curled head into a shaft of moonlight. It was Eliza Elliott who bent over her!

The silent figure in white creaked out of the room, softly closing the door. Ellen heard the lock click into place as the fear fell from her so suddenly that she listened to hear it drop to the floor. She relaxed with so great a flood of relief that her eyes closed and sleep overtook her almost on the instant.

She thought she had reached the third verse of "Sir Patrick Spens" when Sir Patrick unaccountably began shaking her. Bewildered, she sat up to see the first light of the summer morning coming through the windows and to find an agitated Susan pulling at her arm. After that incredible night, she had slept for hours.

Still drowsy, Ellen threw the blanket aside and swung her feet to the floor. "Do stop pulling at me, Susan," she said crossly. "What's the matter with you?"

"It isn't me. There's something wrong with Denise!"

Wide awake then, Ellen ran to the open door of Denise's room. The girl lay heavily sprawled on her tumbled bed. Her face was a dreadful color and she breathed irregularly with deep, snoring sounds.

"She won't wake up," Susan whimpered, "and I shook her hard. I don't think sleeping tablets should act like that."

Ellen didn't either. "Get somebody. Get anybody who'll know what to do. I'll phone Sandy."

Susan ran out and in a few minutes brought back the nurse who had given Denise the tablets. One look at the face of the unconscious girl started her to work. She and Ellen got Denise to her feet and began walking her up and down. They were wet with sweat from the effort of supporting the limp, lolling body when the Doultons, father and son, hurried in.

Half an hour later, the elder doctor sat down on the couch and wiped his face.

"How is she?" Ellen began fearfully.

Doctor Doulton pursed his lips and his bushy brows lifted in answer. "Let's go over what happened— as far as you know, that is." He turned sidewise to face her. "Did you see Prinn give the tablets?" He waited for Ellen's nod. "Tell me just how it was."

He sat silent after she had finished. Then he asked, "You could swear Prinn gave her only two tablets?"

"Of course. I saw her."

"And there were more tablets in the bottle when Prinn put it away?"

"I didn't count them, so I can't say exactly how

many more there were, but the bottle was more than half full." Ellen was firm about that.

Doctor Doulton looked at her, his eyes carefully expressionless, "The bottle's completely empty now. Denise has had a dose that could kill her three times over."

CHAPTER XIV

Ellen knew who would be standing in the hall before she opened the door. Never notable for concealing what she thought, she donned an unconvincing smile for the despicable Dora.

"Dear Miss Knowles again! You've stepped right into the position of family friend, haven't you?" Dora's facile smile and flow of talk turned on like a loose faucet. "How is poor Denise?" The smile was replaced by a look of proper concern.

"I don't think they know yet." Ellen's eyes searched the hostess' face. Now she could see that it all showed dimly there; that devious double-dealing narrowed the bland eyes at the corners and tightened the thin lips when the masking smile slipped. The hidden meannesses disturbed the surface like a dangerous snag beneath calm river waters.

The hostess twitched at her hair and her dress uneasily under Ellen's steady stare. "My gracious, does my slip show? Or are you committing me to memory?" she asked sharply.

Hampton Potts, standing beside Dora and wiping his thick lenses and then his hands on a pristine handkerchief, tittered.

"Use the plural," Ellen couldn't resist saying. "Your slips are showing!" She flipped the waxed tissue-wrapped flowers the man held with a forefinger. "For Denise?"

"Well, no—that is, we mean them for—"

"They're for Charles, naturally," Dora interrupted. "How could we have known anything about Denise's —ah, accident, until we heard about it in the dining room just now?"

"In the dining room?" Ellen asked innocently. "You ate breakfast *there?*"

"Certainly." The hostess' indignation at the insinuation of Ellen's words was a masterpiece. "That unfortunate incident was caused by outside tampering, and now the food is perfectly safe."

"Well, you should know," Ellen said ambiguously, then added to Hampton, "Why don't you take those down to the funeral home? Denise doesn't need funeral flowers—yet. And please excuse me?"

Ellen smiled brightly and closed the door to clip off the woman's words, "Well! I *must* say!" She was folding the blanket on the settee, when Isobel, hollow-eyed and haunted, dropped wearily into a chair. "Have they been out? Is there any change?"

"I don't know," Ellen said honestly. "Doctor Doulton was out a while ago and said for you not to worry. You know how chatty doctors are."

Isobel's eyes searched Ellen's face as if she expected to find the truth written there. "Do they think she will die?"

"Of course not." Ellen could even hear the false

heartiness of her voice herself.

Isobel's gaze dropped to her lap. Growing conscious that she was twisting and wringing her long fingers, she held them still by a visible effort. In a moment she got up restlessly and, with her lurching walk, went over to her plants in the sunny window. She picked off a dead leaf here and there and absently explored the earth in a pot or two with a forefinger. She held one plant to the light and ran her thumb over a leaf, then looked at the thumb closely. She placed a newspaper under the pot and, going to the corner cupboard, opened a drawer.

She stood staring into the opened drawer for a long time. When she looked up there was stark fear in her eyes.

"It's gone," she said in a whisper.

Ellen sprang to her feet and came to peer down into the drawer, too. "What's gone?" she asked unconsciously matching Isobel's shocked voice.

"The plant dusting powder." Isobel waved vaguely at the pot waiting on the newspaper. "The new kind I mixed to try on my plants; the all purpose poison."

"Poison!"

"Of course." Isobel's voice was faintly impatient. "How would it kill insects otherwise? This was a combination insecticide and fungicide; nicotine sulphate, sulphur, arsenic—" Se turned over some small boxes and packages in the drawer. "The nicotine's gone, too, and so is the arsenic."

Ellen mentally shook herself. "You've put them some place else and forgotten," she said matter of factly. "Who would take such things except another gardener like you, and where is one?"

There was a dazed expression on Isobel's face as she turned the packages again. "I suppose I must have moved them," she said slowly. "But where? And why? I don't remember." She rubbed her hands down over her face, and shook her head. "Sometimes I think I'm losing my mind! I do forget so much. No one would take such things." She avoided Ellen's gaze as she shut the drawer and placed the pot back in the window.

It was definitely no time for poison to be missing, misplaced or otherwise. Ellen's thoughts flew to Tom. Where was the man every time she needed him! Isobel went back to her chair. Her hands began twisting together of their own volition while tears fell slowly on the white fingers.

"It's my fault," she murmured as if she thought aloud." I am insane not to have seen it. Mother first. Then Charles knew. Denise—" her voice broke over the name "—was such a darling baby. I used to pretend she was my own child, and I loved her as if she were. We gave her everything she ever wished for, anything her heart desired. So she couldn't bear disappointment. But I didn't think—" Isobel dropped her face into the tear-wet hands.

Ellen's startled heart skipped a beat. She found herself on her feet, but Isobel didn't seem to notice, for she did not glance up. What *had* she said? That Denise had taken the over-dose purposely? She must find Tom, Ellen thought wildly. There was something wrong with Isobel. Maybe she was right about losing her mind!

She was nearly running when she reached the elevators. "Everything goin' completely to pieces aroun' here," Witless began his high-pitched monologue as he assured himself of a listener by shutting Ellen in the car. "Miss Dora, she claim I oughter be call 'Shif'-less,' but I ain't seen it and I tole her I ain't. I gotta keep this elevator runnin' and I kain't keep track of ever' little ole can of somethin' gone out the broom closet. She say she brung a bran'-new can of floor wax up here day befo' yestiday mornin' herself and it's gone now." Witless sighed windily. "I gits the blame for everything and I kain't rightly keep my mind on little stuff when all these sorrerful things is happenin'."

He rolled his eyes at Ellen, but she was deep in her own puzzled thoughts. Witless talked incessantly and suffered the common fate of those who do; no one ever listened to him.

"Shore is some mighty sorrerful things, miss. I grieves for Mista Cha'les; he was one nice gennelmun, he was. Always givin' me and Willie a dime or a quarter ever' time he rode up or down. Miss Isobel'd say he throwed his money to the birds, an' he'd laugh an' say he liked to throw chicken feed to the black birds!" Witless cackled in memory of the well worn joke. "He was talkin' about you, miss, the very las' time I took him up in this elevator. I ain't seen you since to tell you what he said. Mista Cha'les say, 'Witless, be shore to tell Miss Ellen, next time you take her up, to read 'at book.'"

Hearing her name, Ellen looked at the boy in surprise. What was he maundering about? She spoke sharply, "Witless, what *are* you talking about?"

"Yessum, 'at jes' what he say, 'Witless, be shore to tell Miss Ellen next time you take her up, to read 'at book.' Then he say, 'Now don't forgit,' and he flip me a quarter."

"Who? What book? What on earth—?"

"I don' know no more, Miss. Mista Cha'les he say tell you to read 'at book and he done give me a quarter. I ain't seen you since on account of everything goin' completely to pieces. He shore was a mighty free gennelmun," Witless ended on a hopeful note.

Pocketing the quarter she produced absently, he opened the doors and bowed her into the lobby. Ellen walked to the phone booth, trying to recall that last conversation with Charles Chatham. Surely they hadn't talked about books. She could remember something about "pseudo-accidents" and that he had said the successful practise of law required a knack for mind reading. Then he had told her an allegorical story about a boulder on a mountainside that hadn't been clear to her at the time and was even less so now when most of the details had dropped from her memory. She couldn't recall the least reference to a book.

Mr. Ranger had just stepped out of the sheriff's office, but they would tell him that she had called, a noncommittal voice told her. As she came out of the booth Ellen thought belatedly that she probably shouldn't have left Isobel alone. She would hurry back and talk to one of the Doultons when they had a moment to spare.

She had reached the elevators again when the elderly desk clerk called her. He was teetering from heel to toe beside the corner table labeled "Lost and Found" that usually held single gloves, defunct cigarette lighters, and crumpled handkerchiefs retrieved from the lobby chairs. Now it was piled high with a wide variety of unrelated objects.

"Is anything here yours, Miss Knowles?" the clerk asked, indicating the heap. "All these things were picked up on the porches and in the lobby after the—" He paused to choose a word, and Ellen could not resist helping him.

"The Day of Upheaval?"

The clerk smoothed the parentheses of hair that inclosed his bald spot. "Well, yes," he agreed. "I'm asking everyone to look."

"I haven't missed anything." Her eyes ranged over the scarves, the hats, the knitting bags, the magazines, the books— She suddenly remembered that Susan had brought her a book that morning. What had become of it? Maybe the only whodunit in the stack was a tribute to her literary taste! She couldn't remember either the book or her library card number, but it might be hers. She could call Susan about it.

In the elevator she turned the book over and read the title again; "Murder is a Family Affair." When you encountered the real thing, she thought, books seemed slightly academic.

Witless looked interested. "Is 'at the book Mista Cha'les wants you to be shore and read, miss?"

Ellen stared at him. Maybe it was. They had certainly not talked about books, but it was possible that he had noticed this one. That is, if the book was the one Susan had brought her that morning. But why tell her to read it? It looked no different from dozens of others that she could see—lurid jacket; provocative title, "Murder Is a Family Affair." A chilling thought ran through her mind as she tucked the volume under her arm.

Back in the little sitting room, Isobel rocked gently, eyes on her fingers linked together in her lap. She looked up with little change of expression and said nothing. Ellen sat down on the settee and opened the book. She read the first three pages, but so many thoughts pushed up through the words that the total effect was confusion. Whatever the book contained that Charles wanted her to notice would have to wait for a quieter moment.

But she could make sure that the book was the one Susan had brought. Earlier, when it was plain that she could do nothing more for Denise, Susan had gone down to open the library. She answered Ellen's ring with a note of apprehension in her voice and an instant question. When she learned that the Doultons seemed satisfied with Denise's progress, Susan sighed with relief and in reply to Ellen's question verified the card number. Idly turning the pages of the book as they talked, Ellen came upon a small fold of paper tucked deep in the binding. She remarked that the book wanted housecleaning.

"You'd be surprised at the things we get out of them sometimes," Susan said. "Readers mark their places with love letters and gas bills, with hairpins and nail files; anything except a book mark. Once I found a strip of raw bacon! I cooked that for Sugar; ever since she's had a taste for modern literature."

Ellen was staring at the slip of paper she had unfolded. In tiny precise letters she read, *"About our little talk. Sandy had better look into me if—"* Was it a message from Charles Chatham? What he wanted her to be sure and read rather than the book itself? What did it mean?

She looked blankly at the receiver on the table beside her, which emitted clacking noises. She picked it up. "What did you say, Susan? Something drew my attention for a moment."

Susan repeated, "I said I don't see how that book could have stuff in it, for I just catalogued it the day before I brought it to you. It hadn't been checked out before."

"Thank you so much for calling," Ellen told her absently, and hung up. At both ends of the wire puzzled people turned away from the telephone.

Denise was out of danger. Doctor Doulton, coming out of her room as Ellen turned from the phone, took Isobel's hands in his own and told her gently that the worst was over. The girl was terribly weak, but conscious. They had started to work just in time.

"She'll be all right now," the doctor said, patting Isobel's hands. "But what a constitution she's got! Not to mention a remarkable toleration for that particular drug. It's a miracle that tremendous dose didn't kill her."

Isobel pulled her hands petulantly from his sympathetic clasp and turned away. "Perhaps we shouldn't have interfered."

"Interfered?" The word was explosive. "Let me tell you, Isobel Chatham, if we hadn't interfered, as you call it, that girl would not have wakened this side of Paradise!"

Ellen made a tiny negative gesture with her fingers. She shook her head at his raised eyebrows and formed silent words. "I must tell you something. At once."

Near the door of her room, Isobel stood in indecision. At last she raised her head and asked hesitantly, "Could I see her?"

"Just for a minute. Don't talk much."

Ellen followed to the door of Denise's room. She saw, over Isobel's shoulder, that the girl lay limp, her face as white as the pillows, her arms at her sides. Isobel walked slowly nearer. For a moment fathomless violet eyes looked up into inscrutable dark ones. Then dark lashes dropped, the blue-veined lids slowly closed, and Denise turned her head away. With a curiously final gesture, Isobel limped from the bedside without a word.

Sandy followed her out into the sitting room and laid a hand on her shoulder. "She's going to be all right, Isobel. But how the devil did she get that dose?"

"Don't you know?" Isobel's voice was scornful, heavy with hurt. Shrugging his hand from her arm, she went into her bedroom and closed the door. Then they heard the click of the lock.

CHAPTER XV

The three of them stared at the painted panels of the closed door. Ellen marveled that white wood could express so much grief, so much uncomprehending hurt; how the click of the lock could tell of sick resignation and confusion of purpose.

A wordless sigh lifted Doctor Doulton's rumpled, sweat-damp white coat. Sandy turned from the door to confront Ellen. A homely old word her grandmother often used described his expression. He looked flabbergasted. Ellen supposed she did, too.

"What goes on, for the Lord's sake?" Sandy asked in exasperation. "Has everybody gone stark, staring mad? Or have I?"

"You may have the right word," Ellen told him. "Come over here and sit down. I've got to talk to you both." She had to tell them what she knew and what she suspected. She couldn't keep silent without being responsible if anything else happened.

So she told them what Denise had said and how her manner had hinted at even more. Then she told about the intruder who had nearly scared her to death and then worked up to the anticlimax of smoothing her forehead and taking her pulse. Sandy stiffened in his chair and brought his clenched fist down on the chair arm.

"Oh God!" he groaned. "Miss Liz! Making like a Grade B chiller!" He asked Ellen, "Why didn't you scream the place down?" Before Ellen could explain how her throat had contracted with fear, Sandy went on, "I thought all the time it was Miss Liz on the stairs, but she didn't mean to hurt you. Now, Dad, if she's got a pass key, something's got to be done about her."

Doctor Doulton shook his head. "I don't know where she would get one."

"Amy Lou's Dorrie!" Ellen said. "She must have had one!"

Sandy's face was screwed into a puzzled scowl. "Have what?"

"Someone could have taken her pass key from her body."

"Body!" Sandy was on his feet again, almost shouting. "Miss Ellen, are you crazy too? Body!"

"Shut up, Sandy," his father said sharply. "Where does Amy Lou's Dorrie come in? Or her body?"

So Ellen told the whole terrifying tunnel episode, at the last moment remembering to leave out Dora Martingale and Doctor Fowler until Tom and the sheriff got through with them. There was enough shocking force in what she had to reveal to cover any gaps in the story, at least for the time being. Before she finished Sandy was pacing the floor distractedly and Doctor Doulton's cigarette, forgotten, charred a small smoking circle on the carpet at his feet.

"And that's not all," Ellen said miserably, looking up at the two men. "Tom doesn't know this—I haven't seen him this morning. This is about Isobel."

She described Isobel's strange behavior earlier. When she reached the missing poisons the older doctor groaned in consternation and Sandy's pacing stopped abruptly. "And I don't know what this means," she said hesitantly as she tried to tell the rest of the confusing story.

"It means wholesale murder," Sandy said wildly, "if we don't get the maniac responsible! And here we sit on our fannies while—"

"Shut *up*, Sandy!" his father said again. "Let Ellen finish. There's no point in rushing around before we know what we're trying to do."

Ellen told them as much as she could recall of the puzzling conversation with Charles Chatham and Witless' later message from the dead man. Then she produced the folded slip of paper that must be the message, and showed them the book with its ominous title: "Murder Is a Family Affair."

The yellow head and the gray bent over the paper together. Then both men sat back with blank expressions so identical that Ellen was fleetingly amused.

"Now 'Look in at me' would make sense. What does 'Look into me' mean? Nothing! Pure gibberish! Absolute nonsense," Doctor Doulton snorted.

"In other words, tommyrot?" Sandy asked him. "I don't agree. Mr. Charles wasn't a man who went in for nonsense. This means something."

"Get Witless, Sandy." Doctor Doulton chewed his lip in perplexity. "Maybe that sieve he has for a brain caught something else."

"I ain't suppose to leave 'at elevator," Witless protested as he shambled in with Sandy. "Under no condishons, Mr. Sandy. Miss Dora, she'll—"

"Never mind Miss Dora. You just tell us again what Mr. Charles said that morning."

"But I done tole Miss Ellen and it was her he said to tell."

"Tell it again. Tell everything he said to you." Doctor Doulton rattled some coins together in his pocket suggestively.

"Yes sir!" Witless said promptly. "Mista Cha'les he say, 'Boy, be shore to tell Miss Ellen, next time you take her up, to read 'at book.' Then he gimme a quarter. He shore was a generous gennelmun."

"Was that all he said?"

"Yessir, that's all. He shore was a generous—"

"He said that when you took him up to his room after his bath?"

"Yessir, he shore was a—"

"He didn't say anything more about it when you took him down again?"

"When I took him down ag'in?" Witless blinked his eyes questioningly.

"When you took him down at dinner time," Doctor Doulton said impatiently.

"I never took him down no more." Witless shook his head mournfully. "He never went down no more with me. Nex' time he went down in 'at basket on the freight elevator."

The three stared at each other. Ellen tried twice before she could get words past her lips. "Would that make the same kind of symptoms?" she whispered.

Father and son looked at each other for a long moment. Then they both nodded. Sandy got wearily to his feet.

"Come on, Dad. It's plain enough now. He didn't get it at lunch. He suspected something. 'Sandy had better look *into* me'—but we didn't look for that."

Numb with horror, Ellen watched them go out of the door.

"He shore was a generous gennelmun," Witless' hopeful voice repeated the elegy.

Tom sent word to come over to the sheriff's office, go up to the second floor, enter the first door to the right, sit down and say nothing until he called her. Still numb from the morning's revelations, Ellen brushed and braided her hair and buttoned herself into a dark green linen. She noticed when she put on her hat that changing her hair-do had given the peach basket panama a certain dash. Or maybe the change in her appearance was due to the linen play shoes that had replaced her oxford arch preservers.

In the courthouse, she found that the first door on the right was an anteroom of some sort. From the adjoining office she could hear voices; one, rumbling with long pauses, probably the sheriff; another suave with many words, sure to be Fowler's; Tom's drawl, and Dora's torrent. She moved a chair noiselessly so she could hear everything and see a part of what went on through the half open door. She might as well eavesdrop in comfort. And, true to the proverb, she promptly heard no good of herself.

"Miss Knowles was clearly hysterical about the whole episode," Dora Martingale said crisply. "She must have imagined all those lurid details; she simply had a nightmare and walked in her sleep. She's rather an unstable person, I should judge." There was malice in her smooth explanation.

The syrupy voice went on, "Frankly, the whole thing seems rather a tempest in a teapot and—"

It was Tom's voice that interrupted, "You don't consider murder anything more than a 'tempest in a teapot'?"

"Murder!" There was panic in Dora's startled little shriek. "Oh, no, it isn't a question of murder! There have been two most regrettable deaths: one clearly accidental, the other perhaps—ah—aggravated by a most deplorable series of misfortunes. There have been several incidents, unpleasant to be sure, but liable to happen to any public house. Especially in these days of careless, incompetent help and old equipment which it is impossible to replace. We have had a series of misfortunes," she sighed.

"Yes, I think we can describe the deaths of the two Chathams as unfortunate," Tom said blandly.

The suave voice broke in. "Granted that I am as sorry as the next person who did not know them personally that the two Chathams are dead by misadventure, what has it to do with me? Why must I leave my office three times in two days to listen to anybody's opinions about the manner of their death?"

"You'll admit, Doctor Fowler, that there's no love lost between you and the Doultons," Sheriff Anders rumbled.

"But, Good Lord! I don't go around murdering strangers because I dislike their doctors! Don't be ridiculous, man."

Ellen thought Doctor Fowler had a point there.

"I figger you got in deeper and deeper with your fancy tricks at the Eureka," the sheriff persisted. "We found a button from your office coat under peculiar circumstances, remember. And you got them two medicines that was put into the food in your office, too."

Doctor answered with the exaggerated patience one would use with an idiot. "What's queer about a doctor having medicines in his office? Would you indict a carpenter for using a saw or a blacksmith for owning a hammer? And why must I account for every button the laundry mangles off my clothes?" His tone had grown warmer with suppressed exasperation.

"I suggest, Doctor, that you entered into a conspiracy to discredit the Eureka Hotel and the Doultons in order that your own hotel and baths might profit. Briefly, this series of accidents is not accidental; you caused them." That was Tom again.

As nearly as Ellen could see, Doctor Fowler must have jumped three feet into the air and landed shouting. He swore; he yelled; he raved. It was absurd! It was insulting! It was slanderous! Above all it was impossible! And in a suddenly dropped, ominous tone, it was unprovable. Ellen thought it was a most convincing performance.

"You noted that I used the word 'conspiracy.' I have no doubt that you can prove with many witnesses that you were somewhere far away when everything happened, but we know you planned them all, those 'incidents' and those 'accidents.' Your plans were carried out by one or possibly two people actually in the Eureka." There was a pause, and then Tom continued placidly, "By Miss Martingale here, for instance."

Dora's shriek of outrage was a masterpiece. She turned her torrent of speech on Tom and the sheriff. She wept; she called heaven to witness that she had never been so hurt; she cited twenty years of loyalty and tireless service in the Eureka. She challenged them to show that she had ever done less than her very best for the Doultons and the old hotel. She demanded apologies and a complete vindication.

"You can come in now, Ellen." Tom raised his voice over the babble. "Here is a witness who can prove—" He raised his voice and spoke to the hostess. "Will you shut up, ma'am, or will I have to gag you?" Then in the thundering silence that ensued, he went on "—that you two engineered the accidents that have resulted in two deaths. Now you listen. Then you can call your lawyers and sue me for slander. I warn you both, you're going to face manslaughter at the very least."

Ellen repeated for the third time the conversation she had overheard in the tunnel. Doctor Fowler, sitting relaxed and quiet in his chair, kept his unblinking black eyes fixed on her face. Dora trembled and quivered like a volcano on the point of eruption, but Tom's hard eye kept her quiet except for gasps and sighs and indrawn breaths of outrage.

Horror gripped Ellen again as she told of finding Amy Lou's Dorrie in the tunnel niche and as she repeated the words the two had spoken. As she finished, the staring eyes of the hostess flickered and glazed. Probably for the first time in her life, words failed Dora Martingale. She slid out of her chair in a faint.

Doctor Fowler made no effort to help them with the moaning, hysterical woman. He remained in his chair inspecting his well manicured fingers as he linked and unlinked them with a half-smile on his dark face. When the sheriff phoned for a taxi, he stood up and adjusted the creases in his trousers. Then he picked up his hat.

"Will that be all?" he asked in his smooth voice.

"Isn't it enough?" Tom demanded harshly.

"Not nearly enough, my flashy friend." The doctor was smiling, but his hard black eyes flickered over Ranger's tall form, lingering on the boots contemptuously. "And well you know it. It's Miss Knowles' word alone against mine and this lady's." With a polite gesture he indicated the crumpled, weeping hostess now huddled on the sheriff's slippery leather couch. "After hearing of Miss Knowles' fantastic stories and her midnight wanderings, I think any jury would understand that middle-aged virgins often turn venomous when their biologic urge finds no encouragement for expression."

"You dirty devil!" Tom started around the desk. There was rage in his eyes, but his lean face showed only an anticipatory relish.

But Ellen had no mind to have a lance broken in her behalf. Not then or there, at least. She caught at the back of Tom's silver-mounted belt as he passed her and held on. "No, Tom, don't! Look at him! He wants you to hit him so he can say it was all a personal matter! Don't!"

Tom stopped and his shoulders relaxed. "You're probably right," he grunted. He grinned wryly at her, then looked over her shoulder at Fowler. "*Hasta la vista*, Doc!"

"We found Amy Lou's Dorrie in the tunnel exactly like she said," the sheriff went on, paying no attention to their alarums. "What have you got to say about that, Doctor?"

"Exactly nothing, my good sir," Fowler snapped. "You can't prove any connection between me and that darky dead or alive and you know it. So let's have no more of these attempts to panic me. I'm not admitting a single thing. And you won't get me back up here again unless you have a warrant for me—and I'm very curious to know on what grounds you could obtain one. Anything you want to say to me from now on you can say to my lawyers and be damned to you both." And with that the doctor clapped his hat on his head and strode from the room.

Ranger rubbed his chin with a contemplative thumb and looked at the sheriff. "Our little scene didn't pan out like we planned, did it? Likely we should've re-written it. That bird's guilty as hell." He pulled a cigarette from his pocket and the lid dropped momentarily on the eye turned away from the hostess. "Be a pity if he gets off scot-free, leaving Miss Dora here to face the music alone."

The dusty, tear-streaked woman sat up with a jerk. "He's the one who planned everything," she cried shrilly, "and he isn't going to shift the blame to me. I'll tell what he did. I'll tell everything—" The torrent of words tumbled and flowed faster and faster.

"Get that stenographer in quick, Bill." Tom turned Ellen toward the door and gave her a gentle push. "Go on home, sugar. We won't need no re-write."

Ellen went, her head on her shoulder as she listened to the hysterical outpouring. So she bumped into a man standing motionless in the anteroom doorway. It was Hampton Potts. He didn't seem to see Ellen and he certainly didn't hear her apologies. With a sick look on his round face, he listened to Dora's words. Ellen remembered a miserable bumblebee she had once seen on a cold morning, covered with frost, too numb to fly and too confused to crawl.

CHAPTER XVI

The inquest was under way when Ellen crowded into the small room where every seat was filled. She would have been obliged to stand if a tall individual with a vaguely familiar face hadn't silently insisted that she take his chair. She craned around shoulders and heads, but saw no one she knew.

The tubby little man with the air of distracted importance was undoubtedly the coroner. Ellen, who knew her "Alice" well, smiled at his resemblance to the White Rabbit when he pulled a watch from his pocket and glared at it. She was prepared for him to call upon his fur and whiskers to attest that it was getting late, but he announced instead with annoyed testiness that two of the important witnesses were tardy: the Doctors Doulton.

Ellen shuddered. She knew what was keeping them. The coroner and the coroner's court would not wait, the jury was told, because the report of the autopsy on the body of Charles Chatham was at hand. Possibly the tubby little man said with heavy sarcasm, the two doctors would see fit to honor the court with their presence before adjournment.

As Ellen craned to see the jury, she caught the eye of the juror on the end. He instantly grinned and winked with an enthusiasm that dipped plastered hair, bandit-like eyebrows and the toothpick in the corner of his mouth like a salute. Startled, Ellen glanced on either side to make sure she was the one for whom the amazing contortion was intended, but she met only the interested gaze of a bobby-soxer and a wedged-in fat man. The juror continued his pantomime. Looking at the coroner, he held his nose with a fastidious air, then swept his hand down into a gesture. Ellen recognized him then. It was that Doulton partisan, Harry of the Hamburger Hut. She beamed at him in complete accord.

They would proceed to establish the cause of death, the coroner continued. That was the purpose of an inquest, Ellen knew. Tom had told her that before the one held after the death of old Miss Sara. Importantly, the coroner read through a droning jumble of medical terms.

The court then proposed to show that Charles Chatham had not died from natural causes. Clinic doctors, nurses, waiters, and recovered guests followed in a steady stream of evidence that proved the food at the Eureka on the day in question had caused severe and sudden illnesses. Such illness, complicated by the peptic condition of the deceased, had proved fatal, the coroner summed up to the jury. Ellen sat up in surprise. He didn't know about the insecticide!

The coroner expressed more annoyance with the Doultons. The wedged-in fat man eased himself in his creaking chair and murmured to Ellen, "Doc Hamish acts like he's got it in for Sandy and his pa, don't he?"

Ellen nodded in agreement and whispered, "Isn't it his duty to be impartial?"

"Doc Hamish works for Fowler," the fat man grunted as if that explained everything.

The coroner thumped his desk to emphasize what he had just said. If the Doultons had presented themselves, the court could go into the cause of that wave of illness. Whatever emergency had detained them was probably not great enough to excuse this disturbance of the routine required by law. It would be necessary to continue the hearing.

Amid a sudden shuffling at the doorway, Ellen saw Sandy making his way through the crowd, followed by a drooping Witless.

"It's about time you saw fit to honor the summons of this court," the tubby little man snapped. "Now with no more delay, swear the witness, and without preliminaries what caused the illness among the guests at the Eureka on the day in question?" The coroner got it all out in one breath.

"A large amount of croton oil in the chicken gravy and an emetic in the iced coffee."

Surprise rippled over the rows of faces like white caps cresting on breaking waves. The audience had plainly expected nothing more exciting than ptomaine.

"Croton oil? An emetic?" the coroner stuttered. "How did that get into the food?"

"Obviously it was mixed in before serving by someone in the kitchen."

"Could it have been accidental?"

"Certainly not. Kitchens do not use such things for seasoning."

"But the foreign substances placed in the food that day and eaten by Charles Chatham placed such a strain on his system, weakened as it was by a condition of peptic ulceration, that they caused his death?"

"No, they did not," Sandy said wearily.

The coroner's mouth hung open a little. The wave of surprise and excitement washed audibly over the room. "Did I understand you to say—" Doctor Hamish stammered. "But the report of the autopsy—"

"The report that you have there, sir, is incorrect. We have just learned that Charles Chatham did not eat any of the contaminated food that day. His death was caused by arsenical poisoning."

There it was, Ellen thought. The suspicion had become certainty. The coroner hammered viciously for order as the buzz of surprise swept louder and louder over the room like a tidal wave. His face was flushed and angry.

"Why was I not informed of this? Why was an incorrect report given me to be placed in evidence?" His tone indicated that Sandy was in for a bad half-hour.

"To the best of my knowledge, at that time, the report I gave you was correct." Sandy looked straight at the coroner. "I have just now completed the tests that show Charles Chatham died of arsenical poisoning."

"Am I to understand that you did not make the

tests that show the presence of arsenic in the first post-mortem?"

"That is true; I did not make the tests then."

"But you have just now completed the tests and found arsenic in Charles Chatham's body?"

"Yes."

The coroner pounced then. "Why did you not make the tests the first time? Did you not attend the deceased as his physician and have every opportunity to observe his symptoms?"

Sandy raised his voice defensively. "I didn't make the Marsh test because I had no reason to suspect poison'ng of that kind. After all, poisons aren't common in general practice! And the symptoms of arsenical poisoning are often similar to those of common illnesses."

"How much arsenic did you find in the body of the deceased?"

"I can't say with extreme exactness." Sandy thought a moment. "A great deal; certainly a measurable quantity."

"How much was swallowed?"

"I have no idea," Sandy answered. "For so much to be found after an illness lasting several days and with all the eliminations that took place—the dose must have been far more than enough to cause death."

"You say you found nothing in your first post-mortem to even suggest arsenic?" the coroner repeated incredulously.

"No." Sandy paused and then went on. "I think it's safe to say there is nothing in post-mortem appearances

to distinguish arsenical poisoning from a severe diar-
rhea. By the time Charles Chatham died we knew
about the oil and the emetic that caused the wave of
illness. It was only natural to assume that his illness
had the same cause. In his case I knew about his peptic
ulceration and I maintain that there was nothing that
did not fit the picture of severe nausea and diarrhoea
as complicated by his condition."

"And so you neglected to test for poison?" the coroner asked.

"You can call it neglect, if you like," Sandy retorted. "If you found fifteen people with gunshot
wounds and a sixteenth dead beside the others and
exhibiting a gunshot wound also, would you suspect
that the sixteenth was dead of leprosy? That was my
position. Still, I suppose I should have made the tests
immediately."

"Why and when did you get this late inspiration to
make the test for arsenic?" the coroner demanded.

"We discovered that Mr. Charles did not go down
to the dining room for dinner that day and so couldn't
have been affected by either the oil or the emetic.
Then we learned that some arsenic was missing, so I
made the tests. With the results as I have told you."

There was a great deal more of it, with the coroner
hammering away at the symptoms and the treatment
that Sandy had given, but Ellen did not listen. It was
rough on Sandy, with the coroner doing his best to
make him look negligent or careless or both. It might
well be the final straw that broke the back of the
young doctor's practice, already groaning under the

weight of rumor.

Apparently the coroner was going to question poor Sandy all afternoon and there would be Witless to follow him. Ellen grew tired of waiting to hear that Charles Chatham's death was homicide by a person or persons unknown. She slipped out, giving her chair to an avid matron dangling a languid baby.

In her sitting room Isobel sat looking at a book with dull, unseeing eyes while an electric fan droned a song of summer heat. She glanced up and spoke briefly. Yes, Denise was resting well. She would be able to get up tomorrow. Yes, it would be all right for Ellen to go in for a few moments. The nurse was having an hour off, but she had said—

"Is it Miss Ellen?" Denise asked from her room. "Please tell her to come in."

"You see?" said Isobel. "She's doing remarkably; I'm so relieved." But the smile around her mouth did not reach to the brooding black eyes.

It was hard to believe that Denise was the same girl who had lain so wan and limp only that morning. Clear color had crept back to her cheeks and the violet eyes were deep in color like rain-washed flowers.

When a silence followed Ellen's last remark, the girl looked furtively at the half open door and whispered, "Do you think Isobel can hear us?"

"I don't believe she could at this pitch." Ellen lowered her voice, too. "But I don't have the least idea she's trying to, either."

"You go on talking out loud about something or she will think it's queer."

Ellen snatched at the first thought that came into her head. "Do you know that I've never been sick in bed a whole day in my grown-up life?" She pitched the remark a trifle louder than her usual tones.

"Who do they think gave me the overdose?" Denise barely moved her lips.

Ellen shrugged and spread her hands in pantomime. Aloud she continued, "I've had a project in mind for years that I intend to pursue if I'm ever flat on my back."

"Was it the nurse?"

"It couldn't have been," Ellen whispered. "I watched her give you two tablets, no more."

"Susan?"

Ellen stared her surprise at the question and said in a huff, "Maybe I gave it to you myself!"

The violet eyes filled with ready tears. "Don't be angry with me." Denise's voice broke. "You can't imagine how awful it is to know that someone wants to kill you. I've no one I can turn to, Miss Ellen. You've got to help me! Talk out loud some more," she added.

"I have the most elaborate family tree planned," Ellen said loudly. "I have all the material on hand to paint it, too. Had you suspected me of being an artist?"

A gleam of calculation shone in the girl's tear-wet eyes. "Could it have been Cousin Dora? I know she's up to something, creeping and prying."

Surprised, Ellen asked aloud, "Who is *Cousin* Dora?"

"Sh!" Denise cautioned her. "Why, Dora Martingale, of course. Didn't you know she's a cousin of ours? Her grandmother was our grandmother's sister. Didn't you notice that she always called Grandmother 'Aunt Sara'? She never has really liked any of us."

Ellen sighed wearily. What wheels within wheels! Still, what actual difference did it make that the Chathams were kin to the traitorous Martingale? It only made things a little more unpleasant. And what a choice of words that one was!

"I could make myself useful by bringing up your supper tray," Ellen said aloud, but the girl refused to be diverted.

In a louder voice, Denise said, "I'm sure you're capable of being anything you like, Miss Ellen, artist or anything else. I never thought of making a family tree. Ours is so complicated I'd need a very large canvas— or won't you show the dead branches?"

"I'm planning to indicate them by graying the colors to give a somber effect. If you left off the extinct branches the tree wouldn't be symmetrical."

Dora whispered, "It was someone in the night, you know."

Ellen felt an irritation at the whispers. How silly they were acting, she and Denise.

"Fingerprints?" Denise whispered.

"The nurse's on the bottle; the glass had been

wiped."

"Then it was she in the night!" Denise whispered in a frenzy of tears. "She brought me a drink, had me drink it all. It was Isobel!"

CHAPTER XVII

Tom had taken one look at her as she emerged shaken and bewildered from her conversation with Denise and prescribed the long-delayed picnic. He and the rapturous Janie bought food while Ellen dressed, but they were impatiently waiting before she could screw up her courage to emerge in the bare midriff playsuit that was another of her reckless purchases.

Ellen wore the flaring skirt firmly buttoned over the shorts and actually only a few square inches of skin showed. But the exposure was in an area long custom had kept covered. Ellen felt actually naked. A third peremptory knock brought her out to Tom's admiring whistle and Janie's observation, "And alla time I thought you was just a nice old bag!"

Her courage thus bolstered, Ellen negotiated the critical lobby with such aplomb that no one would have guessed that she was wearing the first playsuit and the first pair of red shoes she had ever owned. Tom stowed the basket in the trunk and ushered Janie into the front seat with ceremony.

The child looked at him doubtfully. "You mean

you want me to sit between you?"

"Certainly," Tom told her seriously. "That river road is a bad one; a menace to man and beast. And I might need you to help me with the driving." Looking across Ellen as he closed the door beside her, he added, "Besides, I like the one that sits next to me to snuggle a little, and how do I know Ellen would?" He shrugged his shoulders elaborately and went around to the driver's seat.

Ellen tightened her lips in exasperation. Janie giggled and said, "She might try, Tom."

Tom paused dramatically with his foot on the starter. "She just might. Remind *me* to try, Janie."

The look on Ellen's startled face sent the man and the child into gales of laughter. Ellen could feel her own lips curving up at the corners, but she firmly turned them down. After all—! But no one could maintain a pose of quiet dignity on the river road. A series of chuck holes bounced them into each other's laps and a slanting stretch slid Janie and Ellen down against Tom in what was more than a snuggle.

As the meandering border of trees drew nearer through the clouds of dust they raised, Tom said, "Likely we'll have the whole river to ourselves tonight. Only crazy people put a car over a road like this."

His words were punctuated by a slam as the springs hit the axle. Ellen bit her tongue excruciatingly. Then the road decanted them to the river banks and Tom shut off the engine.

Heat and dust and noise vanished. The river mir-

rored the western sky, in rosy ripples flowing over
shallow ledges to cream into foam drawn out by the
current into lacy scallops. Rustling cottonwood leaves
and the murmurous falling waters played an accom-
paniment for the soaring cadenzas of tree frog and
locust.

Tom and Ellen sat on the bank for long moments,
watching Janie paddle and splash in the shadows. She
could feel the knots of nervous tension loosen until she
felt as relaxed as melting ice cream.

"Why doesn't someone tell somebody about this?"
she asked dreamily. "Hamp Potts can't be a very good
Chamber of Commerce secretary. I didn't even know
he was one till today. He should get this road fixed."

"Typical of small towns," Tom said, skipping bits
of shale to make Janie squeal and jump. "Beller like
bulls, hire space in the papers, think up another something for a silly girl to be queen of; and overlook the
only unique thing they have." He looked at the water
purpling in the twilight. "Kinda pretty, huh?" Then
he got briskly to his feet and pulled Ellen to hers.
"Janie!" he called. "Come out and help us hunt wood.
I'm starving to death."

As he squatted on the high heels of the oak leaf
boots, swabbing the steaks with barbecue sauce, Ellen
told him about the conversation with Denise. When
she had finished, he said succinctly, "Nuttier than a
pet coon."

"Who? Isobel?"

Tom shook his head. "No; Denise."

"But, Tom, she said Isobel gave her the overdose!

She said that Isobel brought it to her in the night!"

Tom shook his head again, unconvinced. "Isobel loves that girl, so how can you believe that yarn? And I don't know why Denise would tell it. You'd better round Janie up; these steaks are gettin' done fast now."

Janie had gathered wood in the nearer reaches of the trees, ranging like a happy puppy, but the warm shallow water was irresistible. Even her red hair ribbon was soaked as she ran through the ripples and then sat down in a mighty splash as her feet flew out from under her on a spot slick with moss.

"Come on, Janie. Supper's ready," Ellen called.

"Come get me. I want you to wade too." Janie skittered off again like the black water bugs.

"I don't want to get as wet as you are." But Ellen was tempted.

"Take off that ole skirt. I won't splash you, cross my heart."

Ellen hung the flaring skirt on a limb, stepped out of the red shoes and waded in. The current purled around her feet as she picked her way across the shallows to the child, flat on her stomach, splashing and blowing like a strangled porpoise. Janie scrambled to her feet with a surge of the creaming water.

"If you'd hold my hands we could walk on the rocks."

As Ellen grasped the wet fingers, she asked, "What are we going to do with you, child? You can't ride home like this; you'd catch cold."

"I could wear your skirt," Janie was ready with a solution as she looked up at Ellen. "You look swell in shorts, Miss Ellen. Most ladies stick out too much in the back. I betcha Tom will—"

"I betcha Tom will starve to death if you two don't quit paddlin' in that water and come eat." His figure was shadowy on the sandy bank, his face lit by the glow of a cigarette. "Janie, you're wetter than ten pounds of catfish!"

"I'm going to wear Ellen's skirt. You turn your back, Tom," Janie ordered, climbing out on the bank and stepping out of her wet clothes. A small glimmering whiteness in the dusk, she pulled the skirt from the branch and backed up to Ellen. "See, I'll stick my arms through the pocket holes and you tie the belt around my neck."

"Are you decent?" Tom asked with great seriousness, then turned around. "You'd better scamper over to the fire to make sure no hungry coyote snaps up those Grade A sirloins."

As Janie ran ahead, he stretched out his hands to Ellen. When she laid her fingers in his clasp Tom pulled her up the bank with enough force to bring her into his arms. For a moment Ellen stood close enough to the brown gabardine shirt to feel the thudding heart beneath it. Then he lifted her chin with a finger and kissed her hard and long.

"Mm, nice," he said in a matter of fact voice, releasing her with a light spat on the part that didn't stick out too much. "Here are your shoes, sugar."

As she walked back to the fire, her hand lightly held in Tom's, Ellen thought how right her grandmother had been. Exposure, decent or otherwise, did lead a man on.

When the steaks were reduced to bones that a hungry hound would have scorned, Tom built up the fire and started Janie roasting marshmallows. As he sat back on his heels smiling at the child and whittling thin sticks for her, Ellen watched the play of the firelight over his face. She noticed the high cheek bones, the straight mouth; saw the laughing quirks at the corners of his eyes deepen at something Janie said. She admired the strong column of neck under the open shirt collar, the easy lift of long muscles, thin brown fingers that hinted at an inner sensitiveness denied by the hard surface sum total. When his eyes caught her gaze, she turned away, coloring in spite of herself.

Tom thrust the last of the thin, bending sticks into the ground and plugged a marshmallow on it. "Now all you have to do is watch and touch it once in a while so it will bob and turn another side to the heat," he told Janie, rising from his crouch with one motion. Crossing to Ellen's side, he sat down with his back against the rock she leaned against and changed her position so that his arm and shoulder supported her instead. Then, bending one long leg at the knee and stretching the other out, he sighed with satisfaction.

They had watched the dancing flames for a long time when Ellen turned slightly so she could see his face. "Tom, is it over, do you think?"

He pulled a cigarette from his shirt pocket and lit it with one hand before he answered her. "I hope so. We got a break when you overheard that nasty pair in the tunnel." He smoked in silence for a while and then went on, "That's mostly what cops do, you know: put on the pressure and wait for a break. Only lots of times we aren't smart enough to see the break when it comes."

Across the fire, Janie poked the last marshmallow into her mouth and licked her fingers. "She's fuller than a duck in June bug time," Tom said, grinning. Raising his voice, he told the child, "Sling that knot on the fire, puddin', and come over here. I got another arm to hold another girl."

But Janie curled up beside Ellen. "I am hurt; I am jealous," Tom said fiercely. "I am cut to the heart that you like Ellen better than you do me."

"I do not like Ellen better, but she's nicer to lean against. She's softer." Janie sighed. "And I'm awful full and sleepy."

While the fire died down to gleaming coals, Janie slept huddled in Ellen's skirt.

Late the next afternoon Ellen reclined steaming in her hot bath. Surely it was time for the bath attendant and the cup of ice water. She felt that she had been stewing and steaming for nearly the proper interval. When she heard the slap, slap of paper slippers on the rubber matting she thought drowsily that her sense of time was very good. She drank the water gratefully and smiled her thanks.

It was Bella, the masseuse. She was filling in, she said, "because I haven't any ladies ready yet. Some are coolin' off and will be done directly." The woman expertly slapped another cold towel on Ellen's head and said in her soft voice, "You look sleepy, ma'am."

"Sleepy as a one o'clock class," Ellen said, yawning. "Be sure you wake me up when you come back. I don't want to do any overtime in this stew pot."

"Don't go to sleep, ma'am." The voice was faintly anxious. "Too many folks goin' to sleep here and not wakin' up this side of Jordan."

"Go on, Bella, I was just fooling."

"Not lucky to fool about some things," the woman said darkly as she went out of the archway.

In a minute or two Ellen heard her come back in. Through half opened eyes, she saw that the attendant stood a little behind her at the end of the tub, wiping her face with a towel. I'd hate to have her job, in this steamy place all day, Ellen thought. Her eye reported a point of the woman's anatomy she had not previously noticed, but her drowsy brain was not interested. "Did you forget something?" she asked sleepily.

The towel dropped from the woman's hand. It fell across Ellen's shoulder as her wet turban was pushed across her eyes. Before she could raise a hand to brush it back, the towel on her shoulder whipped around her throat and tightened. She clawed at it in astonishment and strained futilely to reach the hands that pulled it relentlessly closer. Bella was choking her!

Ellen could not force the scream that grew in her throat past her lips. Red flames shot through the darkness that covered her eyes and her lungs heaved in her chest. She found the hands that choked her and tugged at them feebly as black waves of unconsciousness washed over her brain. Slowly, slowly, she slid down in the deep tub.

CHAPTER XVIII

"If the plumber had come to fix that drain when he was called, it would have been exit for Ellen," Tom told her severely.

Ellen's throat ached and her head throbbed stubbornly from the bump, but she felt very much alive lying on her bed in her best housecoat. She looked around the room, her eyes touching the familiar furniture, the curtains swaying in the breeze that quickened toward sunset.

Her eyes came back to Tom's face. How wonderful that its brown angular lines could still mean— "How wonderful, period," she murmured thankfully. Then she listened to what Tom was saying.

"You must have slid far down in the tub and your feet would naturally come up so you tripped that drain lever. It works so easy; Bella and Amy Lou said they were always letting the water out accidentally. They kept telling Martingale to get the plumber to tighten it up."

"How did you get there so quickly, Tom? Where were you?"

"Just stepping out of my bath. I'd got a towel

twisted around me when I heard Janie coming shrieking like the Limited on a rainy night. Bella had run
out into the women's lobby, and Janie heard her and
came after me." Tom turned Ellen's hand over in his
and traced the lines that crossed her palm with a forefinger. "I'm going to see that Janie never wants for
another ice cream soda! Anyway, she tore through
our side like a yearlin' cyclone. And then we both
kinda upset the ladies."

Tom looked up to grin at her. "Only it wasn't
funny then. The girls were getting out of their tubs
and the place was knee deep in hysterics. So the only
way we could find you was to look in every bath."

Ellen laughed at her mental picture of Tom scat-
tering consternation among the unclothed, screaming
bathers. But it hadn't seemed funny to him searching
frantically for her, she thought contritely.

"I could see you weren't dead, so I wrapped you
up in a sheet and brought you on upstairs." Tom examined her hands with close attention and Ellen could
feel her face getting red. Wrapped her up! "Time I
felt like I could leave you with Sandy, whoever it was
could have been over in the next county."

"Didn't anyone see her walking in and out?" Ellen
asked. "Only it didn't necessarily have to be a 'her'
either," she added thoughtfully.

"Sure, a few women on the cooling couches, but
they didn't think anything about it. Why should
they? They saw a bath woman in a wrapped around
sheet with her head tied up, and mopping her face
with a towel, so what was there any different? When

she had you choked and fixing to drown, she walked back to Fifteen, crawled out of the window—you can't see it, remember?—dropped the sheet and towel on the ground where we found them and that was that."

"I'll never complain at the size of a plumber's bill again," Ellen smiled.

"Nor holler when they don't come when we call them," Tom added.

"Then nobody saw a thing that looked queer?"

"Not a thing. That is, if you leave me out, tearing around in a towel for an hour before I noticed! Denise was sunning in a chair on the side balcony upstairs, but she didn't see anyone come from the back. As she said, she was drowsy and probably dozed some. In fact, she was asleep when I came charging up the stairs. I scared her, and when she tried to jump up quick, her slacks and the sleeves of her blouse caught. Those fold-up chairs can bite you like a dog. And we had the devil of a time. She was half-hysterical and hollering, and I don't know for sure if she ever did really get what I asked her."

Tom moved to lean on the foot of the bed and looked at her anxiously. "Let's take you over to Susan's, huh? Looks like the more deputies the sheriff puts here, the more things happen to you. Sandy says you're all right, only your throat will be sore tomorrow."

"It's sore now." Ellen looked at her watch. It was nearly nine o'clock; the square of the window framed the late summer twilight. "I'll go." She shivered. "I'm not foolish enough to give someone a chance to try, try again. I'll be ready in a few minutes." Then she added tartly, "Now get out of here so I can get some clothes on."

A grin lurked around Tom's eyes and Ellen could feel her own face growing red again. He stood beside the bed a moment looking down at her while the smile grew wider. Then he bent down and kissed her soundly.

"Never mind, sugar," he told her, "I'm willing to make an honest woman out of you!"

Ellen was nearly dressed when she heard the first shot. She stood rigid for an instant with her dress held over her head and her arms automatically finding the sleeves. There it was again. And again. She ran out into the hall where doors were opening and people were calling to each other. Anxious voices matched frightened faces. Ellen ran up the stairs to the third floor to find Isobel and Denise.

They stood in the hall and Denise clutched at Ellen. "What is it? What has happened?"

Ellen could only shake her head. Again the fusillade. And again. It sounded farther away then and she saw that the deputy leaned from the hall window yelling angrily at someone in the street below.

He pulled his head in and said to no one in particular, "Crazy kids! Old wreck backfirin' like a riot gun!"

Ellen felt her very spine sag with relief. With other indignant guests she crowded at the front window to see a load of bobby-soxers make a snappy three wheel turn around the corner. The backfiring went on, mellowed by distance, as people telling each other volubly what they had thought and feared trailed back through the hall.

She smiled wanly at the Chathams. Isobel looked as if she had been pulled through a knothole backwards, an effect which the chartreuse robe she wore did nothing to dispel. The yellow green made her face remote and faintly ghastly. She looked really ill. Denise's blondness was emphasized by the dove blue of her dress, making her hair more golden and her eyes more violet, underscored as they were by delicate shadows. The contrast between the two was cruel.

"It must be what they call the resilience of youth," Ellen marvelled mentally. "Three murders and an attempt on her own life and she can still look like that!"

"Go on back inside, Isobel," Denise said, placing her arm around her aunt's shoulders." It was nothing but some kid nonsense. Try to get some sleep now." She turned Isobel around and pushed her gently toward the door. "I'll be back soon, and Dora said she would be right here if you need anything."

"Where are you going?" Isobel asked the question without much interest, her eyes on Denise looking blank and inscrutable.

"Over to the church, dear. Reverend Benson's expecting me in the study now." She glanced at her watch and then asked in a pleading voice, "Let me ask him to come to see you tomorrow? I think it would help."

"No!" Isobel refused harshly. "Don't tell him to come, for I won't see him! I won't need him!" She did not look at either of them again as she went back into the little sitting room.

Denise looked at Ellen. Then she sighed and, making a little hopeless gesture, closed the door of the sitting room softly. "Maybe I shouldn't leave her," she murmured, indecision in her voice. "She's been so queer all day. I don't know what I'm going to do." She wiped tears from the corners of her violet eyes with her fingers and looked at Ellen again. "Are you all right, dear Miss Ellen? I didn't want to ask you in front of Isobel. She didn't hear anything this afternoon and I thought it would just upset her more. What in the world happened? You must have slipped. I can't believe anyone would try to drown you! But I couldn't get anything coherent out of Tarzan, leaping from bough to bough and beating his breast!"

Ellen was puzzled. Then she realized that Denise meant Tom in his towel. "If it hadn't been for Tarzan, as you like to call him—" she began angrily.

"Oh, I'm sorry," Denise said. "Don't take offense; I didn't mean it to sound that way. Still, I don't see that your big brown detective is doing so hot in solving our little perplexities."

"He isn't my—" Ellen started again. "Tom knows what he's doing," she said with dignity. "I don't think you need to worry. He'll find out who caused the two deaths in your family."

"Does he suspect—?" Denise stopped abruptly. Her eyes fastened on the closed door with a curious intentness. "I'm so afraid, so afraid," she said in a sobbing murmur. She opened the bag she held under her arm and hunted for a handkerchief. "I don't want Tom to find out."

Ellen could think of nothing to say. Denise continued to stand looking blankly at the closed door. Then she roused herself and glanced down at her watch. "Twenty past nine! I'm late."

Denise walked down to the elevators. The doors clanged behind her and the cage slipped downward out of sight before Ellen turned to the stairs and went thoughtfully back to her own room. While she brushed her hair and pulled on stockings her mind revolved around the problem of Isobel. It was pure tragedy to see a woman go to pieces before your very eyes.

Then her thoughts turned to the problems of adolescence as she heard the backfire of the jalopy again. There was just the one pistol-like report, so perhaps the kids weren't deliberately baiting the traffic policeman. She poked her head out of her own door in time to see the deputy plunging down the front stairs. She hoped he caught them; then their parents ought to make them stay at home for a night or two.

Almost immediately afterward a knock at her door told her that Tom was back. Susan and Sandy were with him and the dignified spaniel, Brown Sugar, followed the three to greet Ellen as one of her favorite people.

"We're bodyguards," Susan said with a fleeting smile that disappeared in anxiety. "Ellen, I think Tom ought to have the sheriff put you in jail."

Ellen dropped the slippers she was putting in her overnight bag and turned around to stare.

"I mean you ought to be safe there," Susan explained.

"You've got something, kid," Tom drawled.

Ellen automatically took the slipper that the dog had retrieved for her. "You won't need to worry about me. This is the end of it."

Sandy looked at her quickly, then nodded. "You're probably right. Come on, Susan; let's go see Isobel for a minute."

When they had gone out, with Brown Sugar nimbly rounding the closing door to avoid being left behind, Ellen looked miserably at Tom. "I've remembered something that I wish I hadn't. When that jalopy went by again and backfired, it flashed into my mind and—"

"What jalopy did what?" Tom interrupted.

She told him about the load of kids in the old car.

"You heard another backfire?"

"A minute or two before you came in, but that's not important. What I wanted to tell you—"

"I don't know yet if it is important or not, but you didn't hear any jalopy just now. We passed it three blocks down the street with a flat tire and two traffic tickets."

What had she heard? Fear sprang full grown from

the question. Then Susan flung the door open, her eyes panic-stricken, her voice hurrying and panting.

"It's locked and she won't open it!"

As they ran up the stairs, they could hear Brown Sugar scratching frantically and whining at the door of the Chatham's sitting room.

CHAPTER XIX

Tom gave her a push that roused her. "Run get a pass key from the desk clerk. Susan, take that dog away before she wakes the dead—"

His voice stopped abruptly, but his words hung in the air. Down the hall Sandy struck the door again and again with his hunched shoulder, trying to force the lock. He was still trying when Ellen came running back, followed by the clerk trembling and fumbling to find the right key.

When the door opened, it framed horror. Isobel slumped in the chair by the window, her head turned toward them with an air of inquiry, but she neither moved nor spoke. The dimness of the summer twilight swirled and eddied about the still figure outlined starkly against the square of purple sky the window showed. Tom reached for the switch and the room sprang into view. Glaring light glinted from the gun she held in her lap and showed the blue hole from which a dark stream trickled down her calm face to drabble the green garment.

Behind her, Ellen heard Susan's sharply indrawn breath and the spaniel's whimpering, but no one broke the silence invoked by the tangible presence of Death.

Then Sandy pushed the girl aside and pointed to the sofa under the hall window. Susan went obediently, passing the clerk who hovered in a shocked paralysis. Ellen braced herself and followed Sandy into the room.

After the first look she kept her eyes turned away from the pitiful thing in the chair. She felt nothing, despite the two attempts on her own life, except a kind of remorse that none of them had been able to prevent this tragedy and the ones that had led up to it. For it was plain now, as she herself had suspected and as Denise had feared: Isobel had been the one. Hate and gentleness; violence and calm side by side in the same troubled mind. Was that what the alienists called schizophrenia?

Tom beckoned from across the room. Keeping her eyes averted, she went to him. On a small table beside Isobel's chair lay the suicide note.

"Don't touch it," Tom warned as she bent to read it. "Although fingerprints won't be very important now, I reckon."

The spidery words hurried across the page as earthly time had run into eternity for the writer.

I only wanted a little freedom. All my life I've been tied to wheel chairs, Mother's, Charles', soon my own. Her life had been lived; her years were a burden to herself and to us. That was all I planned, but Charles knew and I was afraid.

I've failed with murder as with everything else. This is what I should have done at first.

Ellen looked at Tom, but she could say nothing. The only emotion she felt was pity.

The room began to fill with people. Sheriff Anders, his booming voice reduced to an explosive rumble, took the hide off the subdued deputy in a corner by the door; Doctor Doulton, his eyes fixed and shocked, joined Sandy beside the silent figure in the chair; a greenfaced youth from the newspaper office edged in and was pushed out when noticed. Ellen was leaving herself when Dora Martingale came, weeping aloud on Hampton Pott's arm.

When Dora asked for Denise through dripping tears, Ellen realized that she was perhaps the only one who knew where the girl was. She tugged at Tom's sleeve, to tell him that she and Susan would go for Denise. A small lighted sign directed them to the pastor's study in the church on the opposite corner of the next block. Murmured talk came from the half open door. Ellen's hesitant knock brought a grave, sedately dressed young man who looked at them inquiringly. Beyond him in a chair beside the desk, Denise sat staring at her hands tightly clasped together in her lap. She glanced up when she saw Ellen and Susan and got to her feet.

Before she could say a word to the minister or more than wonder what she was going to say to Denise, Ellen heard a step behind her. She whirled with a gasp, but it was only Tom looking over her head at the girl with pity a visible message on his face.

"Can I do anything for you people? Won't you come in?" the young man asked, perplexed by their silence.

"No, thank you," Ellen murmured, belated and inept. "We were walking and thought we'd stop to bring Denise back with us. But if she isn't ready—"

The girl's look was intent. "I was just leaving," she said, turning to the young assistant. "Thank you for everything. I'm going to do what you advised. I'll talk to him the first thing tomorrow, and if you'll come by to see Isobel—" Her voice dropped as she added, "Even if she did say she wouldn't need you and wouldn't see you."

Ellen looked away from Susan's horrified eyes. Isobel wouldn't need the young minister or anyone else in the morning.

Denise saw the glance. Her eyes flew from one to the other, suddenly frightened. The violet eyes dilated and her face broke into the tenseness of fright. "What is it?" she whispered. "What has happened?"

Were they all turned to graven images? Ellen felt an irritation with herself, but although words tumbled about in her brain, she continued to stand silent. Tom took Denise gently by an arm and put her into the chair by the desk again, mutely calling the minister to his aid.

"Yes, something has happened," he told her. "I wish I didn't have to tell you this, Denise."

Denise's hands clutched the chair arms as she stiffened and half rose. "Not Isobel! No, not Isobel, too!"

Their faces answered her mutely.

Denise began to sob, tears drowning the violets. "Oh, God forgive me, I waited too long! But I had to be sure. Don't you see that I had to know that she was really—" She sprang from the chair then, her mood changed. "Why didn't you do something?" she demanded of Tom. "Couldn't you see? Why didn't you put her where she couldn't harm herself or anyone else? It's been days and you haven't done a thing! I had to find out for myself. If you'd known your business Uncle Charles would be alive. You and that county sheriff!" She had worked herself into a bitter fury as she shouted at Tom. "Flirtatious old fool! Middle-aged moron! Grandmother and Uncle Charles and now Isobel! If I'd had a little more of your protection I'd be dead, too!"

She turned to huddle against the wall, covering her face with her hands while her whole body shook with sobs. Tom tried to pat her shoulder with a soothing hand, but she jerked away from him sharply. Mutely he implored the minister or Ellen to do something, but before they could, Susan took the weeping girl in her arms and, drawing her down to the couch, murmured to her.

The others watched in troubled silence. After a time the minister said softly to Tom, "I must tell you that Miss Chatham feared this—or worse. She came tonight to ask my advice as you must have guessed. She seemed to think her aunt was loosing her mind. She intimated that the aunt was responsible for the death of the grandmother and the uncle. She seemed to believe that her aunt might even threaten her. I told her she must see the sheriff and the other proper authorities at once. For her own protection, if she was right."

"I guess she was right," Tom said wearily. "Like

she's right in blaming us. Only she can't blame me more than I blame myself."

Ellen lay back in the deck chair looking at the stars as they wheeled across the night oblivious to murder and misery on the insignificant planet far below them in space. She felt a relaxation so great that her very bones sagged to rest. If Tom didn't come back very soon, she would be asleep or at least too sleepy to talk.

She should have waited for him in the lobby but she couldn't make the effort. Any shreds of reputation she still retained would simply have to take it. She would rest a little while in the quiet darkness of the side balcony and hear what Tom had to say and then she would sleep the clock around. Tomorrow, she told herself firmly, she would pack and go home. Enough was definitely enough.

Someone was walking down the hall toward the door that opened on the balcony. "Ellen?" Tom's voice asked softly.

When she answered, he flipped his cigarette away in a glowing arc and dropped into the chair beside her.

"Lordy, Lordy, it sure takes the starch out," he murmured. "I'm limper than boiled greens."

Ellen knew exactly how he felt. "Everything all right at Susan's?"

"I guess so. Quieter anyway. Denise was requiring considerable attention from Sandy." There was a note of dryness in Tom's voice. "Susan was waiting up for her—inside."

"Tom, don't you like Denise?"

"Why, I never thought much about liking her. She's an almighty pretty girl."

"Would you want to marry her?"

"Ellen, for the Lord's sake! I'm old enough to be her father."

"I mean, would you if you were at the marrying age?"

"What makes you think I'm not at the marrying age? But I don't believe I would." Tom stopped and thought about it. "Beauty's only skin deep, they say, and the way she can lay into a person with that sharp tongue of hers, I might be tempted to skin her sometime. Then what'd I have?"

Ellen felt obscurely pleased as if she had proved something to herself. Just what she wasn't sure. Tom's chair creaked as he shifted to slap at a humming mosquito.

"Brown Sugar doesn't like Denise either," Ellen said absently, "But she did like Isobel."

Tom grunted in derision. "You still believe you can't trust people dogs don't like? They can get fooled just as fast as we can—not to mention not having quite the same outlook on morals."

They sat in silence for a time, Tom slapping at mosquitoes and Ellen deep in dismal thoughts. Then she voiced one of them. "Tom, do you think this will ruin the Doultons?"

"Not likely to. People are funny. A lot of them get some kind of kick out of being associated a little and at a safe distance with crime. Like the Doultons aren't willing to prosecute dear Miss Dora."

"She's gone already, didn't you know? Sandy told me. Hamp Potts is marrying her tomorrow and they're going some place down state—I've forgotten where —to live."

"Potts is marrying that—that—?" Tom couldn't find a word suitable for Ellen's ears.

"Sandy said Hamp puts the entire blame on Fowler. He takes the position that Dora was too credulous; that Fowler used her as an innocent dupe."

Tom snorted.

"I think so, too," Ellen said. "Sandy said Hamp didn't believe what he was saying either, but he was standing by Dora and she was a pathetic mass of gratitude."

"Love; it's wonderful."

Again there was silence on the balcony. "Don't you have to reconstruct the crimes or something, Tom?" she asked at last.

"That's mostly done in books." His voice was drowsy. "I'd feel kind of silly trying it."

"I mean how do you think she did everything?"

"Not much good guessing about it, for we'll never know for sure."

"And I still don't see why she did."

"Denise said she heard Isobel threaten old Miss Sara if she wouldn't let her go East to some doctor there she thought could help her. Isobel, I mean." He stretched in the creaking chair. "Maybe she worked out the bath accident after her mother refused her. It's plain that she got onto the mess of stuff Martingale and Fowler were cooking up and figured they could be blamed for the drowning. That is, if it ever came out that it wasn't purely an accident."

"She didn't put her mother in her bath every day and just hope for the worst either," Ellen took up the reconstruction herself. "When she got that piece stuck on the tub and sharpened—" Ellen stopped suddenly. "I've just remembered. When I took my first bath I was in Fourteen. A sort of rasping sound came from next door. Tom, that was Isobel sharpening those threads! Maybe with a nail file."

"Could be," Tom said. "And later if she got to thinking you had heard and might remember, as you just did, that would be reason enough for trying to drown you, too."

Ellen went back to her theory. "When Isobel got the sharpening done she probably talked to old Miss Sara about Number One bath being better than Number Fifteen until she got the old lady stubborn. You could see that she would always veto anything that Isobel suggested. Then Isobel took Fourteen. When Amy Lou went by for the second time, Isobel stuck one of those vacuum cup things on the marble partition, used it for a foothold and went over on her mother's side. She was a lot more active than she looked, but she needed some help to climb. The old lady must have been astonished, and that was the murmur of conversation I heard. I can't imagine how Isobel explained it. Maybe she didn't try. Maybe she went right to work. A person's helpless in a bath tub, especially in these where the water's so deep. I think she just pulled the poor old lady's legs up sharply and that's how she got the bump on the back of her head." Ellen felt goose flesh come out on her body as she pictured that savage scene.

"You figure she stunned old Miss Sara first, then frayed the strap and broke it?"

"Of course she did, or her mother would have made some sort of outcry. Still, with all the shrieking and screaming that ordinarily went on, no one would have paid any attention. Some of those women carried on till you'd swear they were being murdered, Tom! In fact, I can't think why old Miss Sara didn't yell her loudest when Isobel came over that partition. She was certainly nobody's fool, and Isobel's actions would have looked suspicious to a half-wit. Well, anyway, when the webbing was broken, she probably held her mother's head under for a few seconds to make sure." Ellen shuddered again at her visualization of the cold-blooded act.

"How did Isobel get back in her own tub then?"

"I suppose she must have had another of those vacuum cup things." Something stirred in Ellen's memory. "Of course she did. I saw the spots it made on the marble in Number Fifteen. So she stuck it on and climbed back over, then probably used a string on it to pull it loose and over. The position of the tub is reversed in Fifteen, so she ran no risk of being seen as she went over the partition. Then she waited until Amy Lou came around again and found the body. She moved fast, and the screw was sharp, so it took only seconds to stun the old lady and break the strap. She could be certain that her mother couldn't survive both the blow and going under the water."

"Then she must have been either going or coming to try getting the gadget off the tub when you met her on the stairs that night," Tom mused. "So she pushed you. Then when you landed in the clothes hamper she put that button in your hand and pretended to rescue you. The button was another fancy touch to implicate Fowler, if necessary."

"Then she brought me that beautiful dish garden." Ellen shook her head wonderingly.

"Perhaps Isobel saw you talking to Charles that morning, the day everyone was due to get sick at dinner."

"She might have seen us. I don't know." Ellen recalled that puzzling talk with Charles on the shady side porch by the baths. "No, she couldn't have seen us. Denise said she was down in the kitchen; that she had been making that 'goodnight fruit.' She mentioned it when she brought me the tray of candy, for there were some pieces of it. Charles ate one of them. Maybe Denise mentioned seeing us talking to Isobel at some later time."

Tom's voice was grim. "Right then was when Charles got the arsenic."

"Oh, no, Tom! She wouldn't have done that! How was she to know that Charles would eat it? Or that Denise or I or almost anyone else who might be with us wouldn't eat it, too?"

"She didn't balk at trying to kill either you or Denise later, did she?" When Ellen had no answer for that, he went on, "She probably thought, with the tray filled with honest to goodness candy, that no one but Charles would eat any of that health stuff. Amy Lou's Dorrie got her arsenic that way, we're pretty sure."

"She was the maid I asked to take the tray to my room when I went to take my bath?"

"She must have been. She couldn't resist sampling some of the candy, and she got the pieces that were poisoned. But don't ask me what she was doing in the tunnel. I can't see Isobel dragging her there. How would she know Dorrie wasn't just sick like nearly everybody else? Maybe she crawled off in the dark to die like an animal will, poor devil. Sandy analyzed some of the symptoms around where you found her and he could identify bits of dried fruit. That's how we guessed about Charles."

"Why didn't Charles tell someone if he suspected his sister? He didn't say anything even after he got so sick, did he?"

The rasp of a match as Tom lit a cigarette sounded unnaturally loud in the quiet dark. "I'm only guessing, but I think Charles underestimated his sister. Like the rest of us. She acted quicker than he anticipated, and when he suspected that he was next on her thumbs down list, he did leave that note in the book for you. I doubt that he cared very much. What did the poor guy have to live for, anyway?"

Ellen remembered her first impression of an eagle chained to a rock. Death had meant release from pain and the limitations of a broken body. She saw again the inscrutable look in those amazing violet eyes. Maybe Charles had been glad to go.

"But trying to kill Denise, Tom! She told me what a sweet little girl she had been, and she seemed to love her as if she had been her own child."

"You can't guess what goes on in the mind of a murderer," Tom said heavily.

He was silent for a moment. "One time I came across a place in the woods where a house had been a long time before. Nothing was left but the cellar hole and some flowers blooming around where the door had been. I remember I picked some to take home to Ma, and she showed me how small the blossoms were and how the colors had faded out compared to the ones like them she had in her garden. She said plants would 'peter out with time.' I've thought a good many times since that families can run out that same way. Maybe the Chathams were running out. I'll tell you what I think, and you can call me an evil-minded he-gossip if you want. I believe Charles Chatham was Denise's father."

Ellen's mouth fell open. She looked at Tom's dark length stretched out in the chair beside her, but she could not see his face.

"Something went very wrong to make the family leave here. Doctor Denis Chatham had a fine practise, Charles a brilliant future; this was their home. Only Charles was a devil with women. I bet you anything you want to name that Doctor Denis caught his young wife with his brother and that was the 'accident' that nearly killed Charles."

"There was a great resemblance," Ellen said slowly. "In Charles and Denise, I mean." Those amazing violet eyes were identical, she thought.

"That's why I think they left here. I don't believe Doctor Denis accidentally shot himself hunting either. Probably suicide."

"And Denise was born in the shadow of violence. I wonder if she suspected that Charles was her father?" Ellen asked.

"If he was," Tom hedged. "This may be all just my evil mind. I don't know one thing that would prove it."

"It would explain many things." Ellen moved so that her hand turned palm to palm with Tom's. His tight clasp was comforting through the talk of murder and violent emotion. "What would they have done to her? I mean Isobel?"

"I'm no doctor, but surely she would have been adjudged insane; sent to some institution."

"Then I'm glad she shot herself. I think she judged herself, Tom, then carried out the sentence."

"You could be right," Tom agreed. "Couldn't see any other end to it, most likely."

He stopped to slap vigorously at the back of his neck. "Let's go get some coffee before the skeeters carry us off," he proposed.

"Tom, I wouldn't go down through that lobby with every tongue clacking at both ends to save my soul."

"We could go down the back stairs here and around the corner and then come back again the same way."

"Where are any stairs from here?" Ellen demanded.

"Right here at the back. Haven't you ever been out here in daylight? You go down into that planting of

roses and you can go out a gate into the alley." Tom
pulled her out of the canvas chair and, keeping her
hand in his, crossed the balcony. "Here," he said.
"Now watch you don't trip; it's darker than a pocket."
He guided her hand to the rail that followed the steps
down into the darkness of the garden, then pulled her
close so they could go down together.

But Ellen stood rooted to the top step. Sheer astonishment made her voice shake. "Tom! Feel the rail!
It's been waxed!"

CHAPTER XX

Wonderingly, her fingers explored the smoothness. Under the impact of that startling fact, her preconceived ideas stirred, leaped and blossomed into new forms like popcorn held over the fire.

"Tom, could we get into the Chatham rooms tonight?"

He was patient and she blessed him for it. "I reckon so, if we had any reason to, but why? I thought we were going after coffee."

"We're going after murder," Ellen corrected him grimly.

She had found what she was looking for by then. In a corner she felt the spraying branches of a big potted shrub, perhaps an oleander. "And Isobel either planted them for Martingale, or took an interest in them when she came so there would be a good reason for asking for them later," she muttered. "Dump this thing on the floor," she directed.

Tom had a pocket flash out, and by its small light she could see him staring at her, but he caught hold of the shrub near its roots and pulled as he overturned the ornamental pot. Something thumped to the floor and rolled in the shower of leaf mold. The beam found a dirt-covered can of floor wax.

"Did you expect to find that?" Tom asked.

"Of course. That was the only quick and easy way to get rid of it. Go on, upset another one."

It took harder pulling, and though she grubbed vigorously the second pot contained nothing unusual. When the third shrub and its pot parted company, she probed a small discolored hand towel and a twisted, nearly empty tube of make-up cream from the dirt. Tom sat back on his heels and, wiping his hands down the sides of his pants, examined the items.

When he looked up, his voice was still considering. "I get it—maybe. Explain it to me sometime, will you? What do we look for next?"

"Slacks, a long-sleeved blouse, maybe a broken plant and a pair of step-ins," she enumerated.

From the corner they could see lights in the Beauregard house. Ellen had looked at her watch as they left the hotel, surprised to find that it was only eleven o'clock. So much had happened in two hours. She and Tom walked rapidly without much talk, having decided that it would take longer to get Tom's car out of the garage than it would to walk the few blocks. Then, too, they wished to arrive in as much silence as they could manage.

When she looked up again, the upstairs windows had gone dark. Susan's grandmother had built her house on the top of a sharply rising hill, and Ellen's knees began to remind her that she had already had a long harrowing day. She clung to Tom's arm and their pace slowed. Then they heard running steps.

Tom looked behind and then stopped. "For the Lord's sake!" he said helplessly.

Ellen saw the little figure flying under the street light then. Janie ran up to them, clutching her side and panting for breath. The red hair ribbon wabbled over one ear and her pajamas were buttoned wrong.

"I couldn't—get out—any sooner," she gasped. "My mama locked up my clothes. She said—everything was over—that you didn't need me—."

"You're mighty right we need you. And bad, Janie," Tom told her rapidly. "Now this is important. You skitter back to the hotel and shut the door of the phone booth tight. Then you call Sheriff Bill Anders and tell him I said to come up to Susan's house fast."

"I could tell him to drive by the hotel and pick me up," Janie suggested hopefully.

"No, no, I want you there," Tom told her. "You sit right there and wait for that phone to ring. I may need to send for some more help."

"And promise, cross your heart and hope to die, you'll come tell me after?"

Tom made the appropriate gesture. "And turn blue and swell up if I lie. Now hurry, Janie."

The little white figure flew along under the light and rounded the corner. Tom sighed and they walked on.

"You planning a little petty larceny?" he asked then.

"I think I can get them without making any commotion. Won't that be simpler? Where will you be?"

"Living room? Upstairs hall?"

"Downstairs is all right, I think," Ellen said.

As they came up the steps, walking quietly, the porch swing creaked and the glowing end of a cigarette moved down. "Hey!" Sandy said cautiously. "What are you doing here?"

They walked over to him and continued to talk in low tones. "Is everything all right?" Tom asked.

"I think so. Denise went upstairs a while ago; she's gotten hold of herself pretty well. Susan's been inside some time. I stayed to finish my cigarette, hoping she would come back out. I wanted to tell her something, but I guess it can wait until morning. Sit down?" he invited.

"No, reckon not," Tom answered. "Ellen wanted to see the girls a minute, if they haven't gone to sleep, and I'll go along and side her."

"You'd better not talk to Denise," Sandy told them. "She was upset when she went in; she misunderstood something—something I said or did—and she was a little hysterical." Sandy sighed. It seemed to Ellen that he sounded embarrassed. "I ought to give her a sedative, but it would probably scare her into a fit, after her experiences with other sleeping tablets."

"Wait for us," Tom suggested. "We won't be long. Ellen won't see Denise if you think not, and then we'll go back to town with you."

"Oke; I've got my car here." The swing creaked again as he sat back. "And tell Susan to come down a minute."

In the living room old Mrs. Beauregard sat distractedly knitting. She looked at them over her glasses, then clicked off the last few stitches, rolled up the wool and speared it with a needle.

"This has been a terrible thing," she said. "I'll never believe again that I understand the human heart. I loved Isobel." She shook her white head sadly. "I keep thinking some of us should have seen it, should have been able to prevent it."

"We all feel that way, ma'am," Tom said. "But remorse is always useless. Maybe we can think of things we did or things we omitted to do that we think might have made a difference, but when a mind is made up to murder—" He stopped and shook his head.

"A thing like this cuts the very earth from beneath our feet, Tom, and the hope of Heaven from our hearts," the old lady said sadly. "I'm going to bed. You feel these things at seventy-five."

Tom laid a detaining hand on the old lady's arm. "Stay with me, Miss Matilde, while Ellen has a word with Susan, and then we'll all call it a day." He moved his thumb in an urging motion toward the stairs.

The upper hall was dimly lit by a lamp on the landing. The first door was Susan's; the next a bath; and the next an adjoining guest room where Denise would be. Placing a hand on the wall to steady herself, Ellen slipped off her sandals. The doors, ajar to catch any breeze, would be no problem. But the beds stood against the opposite walls, she remembered, so the doorway would be a lighter oblong to silhouette any intruder. If she could get what she was after without disturbing the girls, it would be better all the way around.

So there was nothing for it but to get down and crawl to the bench at the foot of the bed; anyone would naturally drop clothes there. A faint rhythmic sound came to her straining ears. While her hands felt over the bench, she puzzled over the regularity of the pulsing, so slight that she felt it rather than heard. Then she realized that the sound was deep, even breathing. The girl, worn out by the anguish of the day had dropped into exhausted sleep! That would make it easier still.

Cautiously moving a knee, she brushed against a high-heeled sandal. It made a whisper of sound, toppling to the floor, and Ellen flattened herself, holding her breath to listen. The regular breathing maintained its rhythm and she reached forward again to the garments. Her fingers knew silk; that was a slip. Under it was the dove blue dress. Then she had it—no, that wisp was a brassiere. Then her fingers found the tiny ridges of elastic sewed into silk; she had the step-ins.

The pencil of light struck her full in the face with the unexpectedness of a blow. She was blinded by the sudden glare. Instinctively she raised the hand holding the garment to shield her eyes. The bed creaked at sudden movement; Ellen heard an inarticulate sound of rage. Then the light went out and the girl leaped upon her.

Fingers like bands of steel clutched her throat, gripping tighter and tighter. While she fought to escape the hands, Ellen thought bitterly that it all came of teaching athletics to girls: "one, two; one, two; up, down; develop your muscles, girls, so if you ever need to choke someone to death you'll be strong enough to do it!" Her lungs swelled in her chest as she struggled for the second time that day. But the roaring black waves of unconsciousness beat faster and faster against her eardrums; she could feel her muscles relaxing in spite of her frantic demands upon them.

One of the hands about her punished throat loosened its grip to twitch the step-ins from her grasp, and Ellen filled her bursting lungs with the blessed air. But she lay like one in a nightmare, seeing, hearing, comprehending the doom that threatened, but utterly unable to move to escape it. Beside her, cat-like eyes saw her heaving chest and desperate fingers moved back to finish the job. Ellen could not summon strength for further struggle. Dreamily, her mind quoted for her, "Tiger, tiger burning bright, in the forests of the night" as consciousness faded again.

Then her eyelids flinched from sudden light and her ears belatedly reported someone running heavily. The pressure lifted from her throat and again she drank thirstily of the sweet air. Through her flickering lashes Ellen saw light streaming in from the hall. The girl beside her was startled into an instant's immobility. It was as if swiftly moving film stopped clicking through a projector and left a single picture motionless and unreal on the screen.

Tom, racing in from the hall, struck the edge of the hooked rug just as the motionless figure galvanized into action and threw the sandal. Its high heel rapped him smartly between the eyes, throwing him off balance so that his foot hit the floor at an angle and the rug, with the devilish perversity of the inanimate, skidded over the waxed floor. He fell with a force that jarred the house. In one movement, it seemed to Ellen, the girl sprang to her feet, vaulted over the bed and slammed into the bathroom.

Vaguely Ellen heard opening doors and voices raised in confused questioning converging upon her. Someone ran lightly down the stairs. Tom struggled to his feet, shaking his head in an effort to clear it. His eyes found Ellen, lying dreamily under a drift of clothing, and focused with anxiety. He got to her in two steps and lifted her from the floor.

"Ellen! Ellen, girl!" He was practically shouting, "Ellen, answer me!"

"You haven't asked me anything yet," she murmured, sounding like an idiot even to her own roaring ears.

Maybe the change of position did it, but she could feel life flowing back into her limp body, impelling her to action. She pushed Tom's hands away and sat up abruptly, her head reeling and spinning. "She's getting away!" Her voice came croaking through her aching throat. "Go after her! *Do* something!" She pounded his chest feebly in vexation.

There was a smile in Tom's eyes as he stood her wobbling on her feet, supporting herself by the bed post. "You're getting back to normal fast, toughie," he said as he ran out.

Like a nightmare, too, everything must have happened in a few seconds. The light thud of bare feet reached the bottom step and the screen door slapped shut as Tom began to yell, "Sandy! Stop her!" Susan flashed by the door and down the stairs, and below, on the porch, the swing banged against the house wall.

Ellen held her rocking head in her two hands and started for the hall, determined to be in at the death. Even if it was her own, she thought grimly. She felt that it well might be, as waves of nausea swept over her. Clinging to the banisters, she dropped down a step at a time, but she was past the landing before her mind could hold more than a blind determination to stay on her feet. Then her eyes registered running forms silhouetted against the lights of the car that was coming fast up the hill; saw the girl stop, then swerve to run into the shrubbery that banked the drive.

During that second of indecision, Susan caught at the girl with detaining hands. Horrified, Ellen saw Denise strike with all her strength, maniacal rage, and jealousy, and fear behind the blow. Susan crumpled with a sobbing cry. Stumbling out into the darkness, Ellen heard more crunching footsteps on the gravel; saw Sandy gather Susan's huddled form into his arms in a panic of anxiety.

As the headlights sweeping around the curve picked them out plainly, Ellen saw Susan stir and then turn, shaken with sobs, closer into the safety of Sandy's arms. What he had wanted to tell the girl, what he had been reluctant to leave until morning, was plain in every line of the young doctor's body as he strained

Susan to him.

The car braked to a stop on the flying gravel and two men tumbled out to run crashing through the shrubs. Beams of light lanced through the tangled branches, and once Ellen saw Tom emerge into the strip of brightness, then plunge out of sight again. Incredibly, a small white-clad figure slid out of the car and galloped after Tom.

Ellen forced her reluctant legs into a shambling run. She knew with despairing certainty that Janie would cut across Denise's path before Tom or Sheriff Anders or the clabber-headed deputy. Her feet felt as if lead weights were fastened to them as she forced her way through the shrubs, not even feeling the sting of the whipping branches.

Then the night was violent with sound. Denise threw herself half over the retaining wall protecting the sharp drop into the street when Janie rose out of the green tangle to clutch at her. Ellen broke through the branches as the child, swooped up in Denise's arms and forced back against the top of the wall, began to scream piercingly.

"Stay back, or I'll drop her over," Denise threatened between snarling lips. "Stay back!"

Ellen moved slightly, and the mad violet eyes caught the movement. Janie slid farther out, the buttoned flap of her torn pajamas catching a cross beam of light for an instant and then merging into the darkness. Behind the leafy screen running footsteps closed in.

Nemesis took the form of a little dog. Brown Sugar,

the spaniel, charged raving and fastened on Denise's bare and lovely leg. Ellen, summoning a last reserve of strength, caught Janie's threshing heels and pulled her to safety as Denise dropped her to kick at the snarling dog. A high-pitched, screaming voice went on and on.

CHAPTER XXI

The scene was straight from the cover of one of one of the more lurid pulps, Ellen thought dazedly. Denise backed against the wall kicking and screaming as she fought off the raging dog. A fragile blue night-gown hung in tatters about her, scarcely veiling the perfect body more than her hair hid the gleaming violet eyes. Her glance flew in desperation from one to the other of the men converging upon her, such maniacal frustration distorting her beautiful face that Ellen turned away sickened.

When she looked again Denise had a jacket flung around her and Tom dabbed at his scratched face with a wadded handkerchief. The sheriff and his deputy struggled with the girl on either hand, but as Ellen watched, the fight and the fury drained from Denise so that she hung limp in their arms. The dog, Sugar, stopped worrying the unresisting ankle and sat back with an air of accomplishment.

"Take her into the house and somebody get some clothes on her," Tom said shortly.

Feeling that she was probably that "somebody," Ellen trailed them wearily, carrying Janie whose sobs had subsided into sniffs. Upstairs, she dropped the child on a bed, where Janie slept almost before Ellen straightened out the briar-scratched legs. In the guest room Denise lay supinely on the bed, too, but her eyes were open, staring blankly at the ceiling. Ellen collected clothing and gingerly approached. When she extended a robe toward her, Denise spat like an angry cat.

"Don't touch me!" she snarled, snatching at the garment. "Get away from me! If it hadn't been for you, you prying old pedagogue!"

"It would have been someone else; you weren't that clever," Tom drawled from the doorway.

Denise sat up in bed, her eyes burning angrily. "Nothing pointed to me! I was safe, but she kept sticking her nose in. I had to get rid of her, too, but I was unlucky. She's so damned durable!"

Ellen felt foolishly apologetic as the girl glared at her.

"What started you in the first place?" Tom's voice was carefully conversational as he lounged in the doorway, one foot braced against the casing. His fingers tenderly explored his scratched face, but his eyes were intent.

"Grandmother was as old as God," Denise said callously, "and still she didn't die. I knew I could get around Charles and Isobel if she was out of the way. She kept a tight hand on our money and she threatened me. She found out I was experimenting with the Pharmaceutical Codex and Doctor Denis' poison cabinet." Denise's voice grew derisive and a sly delight crept over her face. "Grandmother was sharp enough. She didn't have to have the next installment to see what the plot was."

Ellen wondered, appalled, whether the muscular weakness, the pains in the arms and legs that Isobel had suffered and the stomach disorders that had tortured Charles had been due to those experiments rather than to disease.

"But it was all Susan's fault," Denise was saying indignantly. "Little red-headed sneak! She ran after Sandy, sweet-talking him, when she knew I always planned to marry him. I knew he wouldn't rather have her. So I began to look for the reason he wouldn't marry me."

Tom caught Ellen's eyes without a change of expression. She shuddered at the glimpse of the monstrous, murderous ego the girl's words exposed.

"My family was the reason. Who would want to saddle themselves with three cripples? Especially a doctor here? They were only a burden to themselves and to me, anyway."

Where had she heard just that expression? Ellen couldn't recall it at the moment and Denise was going on. That was what Tom wanted; to keep her talking.

"I knew something was biting Cousin Dora. I followed her into the tunnel one night—I don't sleep much any more—and I heard the silly fool being titivated by that gruesome Fowler. Then I fixed it so their little accidents would pay off big. I had to hurry with Grandmother. She'd began to get suspicious about her checks, too, the old miser."

"So you started out by throwing a brick at Susan when you were getting the mastic?"

Denise grinned at Tom's question. "That wasn't so bright, was it? It seemed like a good idea at the time and with any luck I'd have bashed her silly head in." A ferocious expression chased the grin from her face. "Her turn was coming next. I could have made Sandy forget her fast."

"What about Charles?" Tom probed casually.

"When I overheard Fowler and Cousin Dora planning that oil and emetic mess, I saw that it was the perfect opportunity to get Uncle Charles. If I couldn't work it off as another accident it would point to Isobel." Denise giggled. "Isobel asked me to bring her the powdered sugar from our rooms when she was making candy. Any similarity between what I brought and sugar was purely coincidental!"

"That sleeping pill business?"

Ellen could see that Denise was growing restless. Her hands moved over the bed, plucked at her hair, flickered over her lips.

"It was pretty smart, though," Tom added hastily, seeing the restlessness, too.

Denise preened herself noticeably. "I thought that was a good touch. I swallowed enough pills to give me some really good symptoms and put the rest down the commode. I had the time and amount worked out good and careful."

"I guess I'm just dumb," Tom's tone was humble, "but I don't see how you thought it would fool Isobel."

"I didn't plan it to fool Isobel," the girl said tartly. "I planned it to fool you and the Doultons, and how it worked! I was sure Isobel would keep still long enough for you to think she'd tried to kill me and for me to arrange her suicide. After all, she was fond of me."

Again Ellen met Tom's eyes. The coldbloodedness of Denise was unspeakable.

"Then when that backfiring jalopy went by, you saw how you could use it to good advantage?"

Denise nodded. "I changed the suicide to fit it, for it would give me a good alibi, if I ever needed one. When the sheriff put the deputies in the halls, I had to find a different way to keep up with Couson Dora's nightly rendezvous, so I thought about the window-ledge-balcony-railing route I discovered when we used to play cops and robbers as kids. To slide down the rail saved several seconds; besides, it was quieter."

Suddenly Ellen remembered the day Janie had come flying down the banister into the women's lobby. She had seen Denise get the idea right then.

"Why'd you bother to wax it?"

"Well, really, Tom! You should practice deduction; you could use it in your business!"

"And the suicide?" Ellen could see that Tom was beginning to wonder how many more questions Denise would answer. There was a pause before she spoke again.

"I left the door off the latch, so Isobel would think it was locked and it wouldn't be. Then I went down in the elevator, set my watch in the lobby so the clerk would notice the time and walked around the corner like a lady. Then I ran like hell down the alley, through Number Fifteen's window, and up the bath stairs. The deputy was still hanging out of the window, bothered about the jalopy, just as I'd thought he would be. He wouldn't have seen an elephant, but I was careful, and the dress I wore blended with the twilight.

"Isobel was sitting by the window. I changed the latch and closed the door, shot her, wiped the gun on my slip, shut her hand around it, laid out the suicide note I had ready, and went out of the window. It's only three or four steps on the ledge until you can climb over on the balcony, and nobody ever looks up. I found that out when we were kids. I slid the rail, ran down the alley and was in the minister's study stuffing him with my pitiful story at practically the same time I would have been after a leisurely walk from the lobby. No one would ever have noticed the two or three minutes difference."

Ellen forgot to be quiet. "Then back in the sitting room, when you looked so pitiful grieving over Isobel's flowers, you were really brushing out stems and leaves broken off when you stepped over the plants to get out! And latching the screen!"

The restless hands gathered into claws. "*You* would see that! If I'd only pulled the towel tighter around your damned neck!" In a rage she launched herself at Ellen. As her chair went backward with a crash, Ellen's head rapped sharply on the floor for the second time that night.

"But I can't think what made her suspect Denise in the first place." That was Susan's voice she heard as she tried to open her eyes. Tom and Sandy, putting cold compresses on her head, were letting water trickle down her neck, so she pushed their hands away and sat up.

"It was the legs," she told them irritably, looking around the room. Denise was gone; Susan stood beside the bed watching the two men drip water over everything. Ellen's head ached and she felt impatient with them when they looked at her uncomprehendingly.

"When I felt the wax on that railing it connected up with the idea of smoothness and roundness by thought association, I suppose. And that made me remember thinking this afternoon in the baths just before I got choked that I had never before noticed Bella's legs. Whoever was trying to drown me had beautiful long ones.

"And of course beautiful long legs made me think of Denise. It was the very first thing that had, but once you got used to the idea, all the facts fitted her better than they did Isobel. She was out on the upper balcony sun bathing, but she was wearing slacks and a long-sleeved blouse, more clothes than she ordinarily wore around town! I suppose she browned herself all but her hands and face before she came out, and wound a towel around her hair and twisted a sheet around her body. She finished her make-up on the balcony and went down the stairs.

"She peeped into Number Fifteen to make sure no one was there—not that there was much chance there would be—dropped off the slacks and blouse and went in the window. The alley fence is high just to make it surer that no one would see her. Then, wiping her face with a towel, she walked in to choke me. When she thought she had, she went back the same way. She dropped the sheet and went back to the balcony in the clothes. She'd had time to use the towel to wipe her face and hands and stick it in the flower pot before Tom came. She was drowsing most convincingly by that time.

"Then I thought that if she was the one who attacked me, the legs of the slacks and the sleeves of the blouse would have brown make-up on the inside, for she wouldn't have had time to get it off her arms and legs. And I remembered she had talked about scrambling all over the hotel, inside *and out*, so I thought she might know a way to get out of the locked sitting room. If she had shot Isobel, she could get away faster by sliding the stair rail—and what other reason could there be for waxing an outside railing?—and there would be floor wax on the step-ins she wore. Only it sounds much more complicated to tell than to think," she concluded.

"If she had let you alone, she would have been perfectly safe," Tom said thoughtfully. "She could have tossed the panties in the laundry, sent the other stuff to the cleaners, cried gracefully and got the shrubs that reminded her of Isobel. And been clear to inherit the money."

"There's quite a lot of it." Sandy looked sober. "Old Miss Sara had just been talking poor, the lawyer says."

"But like I told you, Ellen, murder will out because of fears. She was afraid of what you knew."

"But I didn't know a thing that didn't seem to point to Isobel rather than to Denise," Ellen protested. "Association of ideas isn't any kind of proof. When I laid my hand on the round smoothness of the waxed banister, that wasn't really reasoning; it was just the way one's brain ties things together so when you pull one idea out another pops up."

"The way facial tissues do," Susan murmured.

Ellen nodded. "Like crackers and cheese; ham and eggs; thunder and lightning; beer and—"

"—and benders," Tom supplied.

"No," Ellen was firm"—and pretzels. And doughnuts and coffee." She stopped with a queer expression on her face. "I *did* know something!" Her voice was amazed. "Only it isn't proof either. Denise was sick, or she said she was, that day when so many were. But if she had been innocent, if she didn't know a thing about the plot to contaminate the food, she wouldn't have been. The oil was in the potato and gravy which she avoided as fattening and the emetic was in the iced coffee which she never drank!"

"She probably didn't think she could escape comment if she wasn't sick," Tom nodded. "So she pretended and tripped herself on an unnecessary lie."

"I was certain Isobel was the one," Ellen said earnestly. "I thought the vacuum cup things pointed to her, just as Denise had planned. When I saw them at the hardware store—" Again she stopped.

"What have you thought of now?" Sandy asked. "I

agree that Denise was right to be afraid of you!"

Ellen didn't hear him. She was looking at a mental picture of a lumpy brown package, fastened with printed, gummed paper tape, "Hardware and Builders' Supplies" repeated down the length of the fastening.

"That was Denise! I ran into her at the door of the drug store the first day I was here! I couldn't see, coming in from the glare outside, and I brushed a package from the hands of a woman just going out. It clanged on the floor and I picked it up and handed it back. It had come from a hardware store!" Ellen finished in triumph. "Denise probably thought I would know her when I saw her again and would remember the package—I'm sure the vacuum cup things were in it—when all I got was an impression of long legs and rudeness!"

Susan's eyes were bright with tears and she leaned against Sandy's shoulder. "I thought of her as my best friend and all the time she was planning—she was—"

"A serpent in your bosom." Tom was charmed with his originality.

"What an actress she is." There was grudging admiration in Ellen's voice. "Not a false note in any of those scenes she staged so expertly."

"Still I remember, now that it's of no use, that I did think it somewhat strange that she always responded to tragedy with rage. I see why; rage is more easily faked than grief." Sandy recalled.

Ellen repeated the question she had asked earlier in the night about another woman. "What will they do with her, Tom?"

He shook his head. "Don't look for much. The deputy took down everything Denise told us—seems funny that clabberhead would be a whip at shorthand, huh?—but she'll deny every word of it. A confession isn't worth much when a smart defense gets to work. And I hate to think how those violet eyes and long legs will work on twelve good men and true!"

"I wouldn't want her to hang," Ellen said. The three looked at her in astonishment. "If she did, Dora Martingale Potts would inherit all that money!"

The banging finally awakened Ellen. Sleepily, she took her bruised stiffness to the door, accepted the envelope Witless offered and found a quarter for his suggestive palm. She sat on the edge of her bed holding the letter until she roused enough to tear it open. A few lines in Tom's handwriting sprawled over the page.

> *Ellen, sugar:*
> *I've got to go in to Dallas this morning. Sheriff says you can leave right after the inquest this afternoon. I'll meet the four o'clock train. You'll make a cute black and blue bride!*
>
> *Tom*

Ellen was furiously indignant. Taking her for granted like that! Not even "Love, Tom!" Black and blue bride indeed. She sprang up to look searchingly into the mirror. Her bruised throat showed shadowy blotches, but it was not noticeably discolored yet.

At the closet she pushed aside the clashing hangers to take down the last and as yet unworn purchases she had made at the ruinous dress shop. The white linen with its handmade eyelets she folded over tissue paper on the bed. In her dressing case she packed the seductive perfume and the wispy white gown and negligee that had lain deep and secretly in a drawer of the marble-topped dresser. The linen dress went carefully on top over the white suede sandals. Then she shut the lid of the case and locked it, muttering furiously. If Tom Ranger thought— What he didn't know about women!

Still holding his note in her hands, she called the desk clerk in the women's lobby. "Could you change my last bath hour for ten this morning?" she heard herself asking. "I'm going to Dallas on the four o'clock train."

www.ingramcontent.com/pod-product-compliance
Lightning Source LLC
Chambersburg PA
CBHW031402250626
47155CB00004B/1384